"I KNOW THE TRUTH ABOUT OUR MARRIAGE," SABRINA SAID ABRUPTLY.

"I know the whole story, Josh—the phony deathbed request, the hurried marriage, the romantic honeymoon in Europe. You and Grandfather knew I'd do anything he asked if I thought he was dying."

Josh hesitated, choosing his words carefully. "I wanted you back so badly that I wasn't willing to question the methods. I felt like you still loved me and I had to take the chance. You know I love you."

Sabrina moved slightly away. "Aren't you confusing love with desire?"

"They're the same thing in your case. I love you and I desire you." He closed the gap between them and reached out to her.

She pushed his hand away. "No, Josh, this time it's not going to work."

CANDLELIGHT ECSTASY ROMANCES®

ENCORE OF DESIRE

Jan Stuart

A CANDLELIGHT ECSTASY ROMANCE®

Published by
Dell Publishing Co., Inc.
1 Dag Hammarskjold Plaza
New York, New York, 10017

Dell ® TM 681510, Dell Publishing Co., Inc.

Candlelight Ecstasy Romance®, 1,203,540, is a registered
trademark of Dell Publishing Co., Inc., New York, New York.

ISBN: 0-440-12367-4

Printed in the United States of America

First printing—April 1985

To Our Readers:

We have been delighted with your enthusiastic response to Candlelight Ecstasy Romances®, and we thank you for the interest you have shown in this exciting series.

In the upcoming months we will continue to present the distinctive sensuous love stories you have come to expect only from Ecstasy. We look forward to bringing you many more books from your favorite authors and also the very finest work from new authors of contemporary romantic fiction.

As always, we are striving to present the unique, absorbing love stories that you enjoy most—books that are more than ordinary romance. Your suggestions and comments are always welcome. Please write to us at the address below.

Sincerely,

The Editors
Candlelight Romances
1 Dag Hammarskjold Plaza
New York, New York 10017

CHAPTER ONE

"Do you, Sabrina Sheffield, take this man to be your lawful wedded husband?"

The solemn words made Sabrina's tilted green eyes widen in panic. She glanced around the hospital room, such a different setting from her first marriage to Josh. She had worn white lace then, her elaborately styled blond hair crowned by a circlet of tulle and pearls. Josh had been waiting at the altar as she had walked down the long church aisle on her grandfather's arm, a look of pure bliss on her face. That was before she had found out the real reason Josh had wanted to marry her.

The slight pressure of his hand on hers made Sabrina realize they were waiting for her response. She looked into Josh's dark, predatory face, mutely begging for a reprieve she knew wouldn't come. There was no escape. She was trapped by her love for two men.

Sabrina's answer was given with a soft sigh of despair. "I do."

After the words were pronounced that made her Mrs. Joshua Winchester, he took her in his arms, holding her tightly against the hard, lithe body that had given her such ecstasy. Ecstasy she vowed never to allow again. Josh's amber eyes glowed like topazes as he lowered his dark head, his warm sensuous mouth covering hers possessively.

Sabrina stiffened instinctively in his arms, fighting the

warm tide that swept through her. She had to remember why they were doing this. If only her treacherous body didn't quicken in memory of the rapture this man could bring.

"All right, you two," Simon Sheffield called from the hospital bed where he was propped up with pillows. "There will be plenty of time for that later."

Josh grinned at the white-haired man. "Don't tell me we're embarrassing you, Simon. You must be getting past your prime."

"Just don't try taking my name off the door," Simon commented dryly. "I'll be back at work before you know it."

He glanced irritably around the large room that could have been mistaken for a suite in a luxury hotel, except for the hospital bed. At the far end was a couch, several comfortable chairs, and a cocktail table. Flowers everywhere brightened up the color scheme of pale beige and brown, a welcome alternative to the usual sickly hospital green.

"Why doesn't somebody pour the champagne?" Simon roared. "The service here is about on a par with the food!"

A nurse in a starched uniform approached the bed. "You positively may not have any champagne, Mr. Sheffield." She reached for his wrist, a look of disapproval on her plain face. "Your pulse is racing already."

"There's no pleasing you people," he answered, disgusted. "Would you rather it stopped?" He fixed her with a glance that had quelled strong men. "And what do you mean I can't have any champagne? My only grandchild just got married, and I intend to drink a toast."

A bubble of laughter lightened Sabrina's spirits as she exchanged an amused look with Josh. The nurse didn't know whom she was dealing with. As chairman of the board of Ameropol, an international conglomerate, her grandfather was used to raising his voice in Los Angeles and having people quake in Hong Kong. He had survived a heart attack that would have killed most men of sixty-six, and he wasn't about to be bullied by a nurse.

"I don't think a small glass would hurt him." Josh stepped in as peacemaker. "I'll take the responsibility."

"But if the doctor . . ." The nurse's protest trailed off in the face of Josh's charm.

"Don't worry, if he comes in I'll swallow the evidence," Simon said cheerfully, once he had gotten his own way.

In spite of the unusual surroundings, it was a festive party. All the floor nurses came in at one time or another to toast the bride and groom. From the sidelong glances the younger ones gave Josh, Sabrina could tell they envied her. If they only knew, she thought despairingly.

A little later Simon looked at his watch. "It's time you kids got going," he ordered. "You don't want to miss your plane."

Sabrina's smooth brow furrowed. "I don't feel right about leaving you, Grandfather."

"Nonsense. I have all these angels of mercy around. They wouldn't let me die even if I wanted to," he said dryly. "I never saw such a bunch of bossy females."

Sabrina bit her lip. "I wish you hadn't insisted we go to Europe."

"It's your honeymoon, child. I want you to take it in style."

"I already had a honeymoon," she answered soberly.

He gave her a long look. "Will all of you please clear out? I'd like to say good-bye to my granddaughter."

When they were alone, Simon patted the side of the bed. He took her cold hand, holding it tightly. "It's going to be all right this time, my dear, I promise you."

"Even *you* can't promise something like that," Sabrina cried bitterly, in spite of her resolve to appear happy.

"Would I ask you to do anything I didn't think was

9

right for you?" he asked quietly. "Don't you know you're dearer to me than my own life?"

She did know, and Sabrina felt the same way about him. She had been ten when she went to live with her grandfather after her parents had been killed in a plane crash. An aunt on her mother's side had wanted to take her, an arrangement that would probably have been more suitable considering Simon's age and the fact that his wife had died many years before. But to Simon it was unthinkable that the child of his only son should live anywhere except with him. And Simon had always gotten his way. He had been right in this case, because a deep and abiding love had grown between them.

"You granted the wish of a dying man." He cupped her cheek lovingly. "It was what pulled me through."

Sabrina gripped his hand convulsively, remembering the terror of those terrible days and nights when it had seemed her grandfather was going to die. Josh had shared the vigil with her, giving her strength. All of their personal problems were put aside—the bitterness, the divorce, her subsequent flight to the East Coast. They were just two people who loved the fallen giant gasping for breath beneath the oxygen tent.

It had seemed like a miracle when he had started the long climb back to health. Sabrina had laughed and cried in Josh's arms, feeling closer to him than ever before. The hours they spent together in the hospital reinforced that feeling, although she knew it was only a temporary thing. She would never let Josh hurt her again. Simon didn't know that, though. He mistook their mutual concern for a reconciliation. He even urged it on Sabrina, who rejected the idea firmly, as she assumed Josh did.

Then came the terrible day when Simon suffered a relapse. He called them to his bedside and made a shocking request. He wanted them to remarry.

Her grandfather's voice was a thready whisper she had to bend down to hear. "I worry about you so, my darling. You're going to be a very wealthy woman when I die, and there are unscrupulous people out there. If I know Josh is taking care of you, I can go in peace."

Sabrina drew in her breath sharply. "Don't talk like that! You're going to get well, Grandfather."

His eyelids fluttered down. "Look at me. You know better than that."

She was terror stricken, but he didn't understand what he was asking. Sabrina had never told her grandfather that Josh only married her to gain control of Ameropol when she inherited it one day. He probably wouldn't have believed it anyway.

She forced down the misery. "Just concentrate on getting well, darling."

"Say you'll do this one last thing for me," he breathed faintly. "I've never begged in my life, but I'm begging now. I have to know you're being looked after."

Sabrina swallowed a sob. "Please don't worry about me, Grandfather. I can take care of myself."

A look almost of annoyance crossed his face, disappearing swiftly. "Talk to her, Josh," he murmured piteously. "Convince her."

Josh's answer was as unexpected as it was hurtful. His sensuous lower lip was compressed in a straight line. "I won't marry her against her will, Simon."

It was said so coldly that Sabrina's heart twisted. It was bad enough that Josh didn't want her—any more than she wanted him, she reminded herself—but how could he talk to a desperately ill man that way? Sabrina would have done anything to ease what appeared to be her grandfather's dying moments, so how could she refuse his death-bed request?

Simon's recovery was as unexpected as the speed with

11

which he engineered her remarriage. He even planned their honeymoon to Europe. Sitting on his bed minutes before she was to leave, Sabrina experienced her first doubts. Had the relapse been faked? Would he go to that length to get what he wanted?

"Trust me, sweetheart," Simon said gently, noting the uncertainty on her face. "And be happy."

Josh was waiting outside the door. His enigmatic eyes searched her troubled face. "Are you ready?"

As she stared up at the tall, lean man, Sabrina could almost feel the trap closing. Under the conventional, superbly tailored dark suit was a stalking male animal waiting to pounce. She had escaped once; could she do it again? Sabrina forced down the frightening fantasy, bringing her chin up. This time it was different. She was no longer the gullible, clinging girl she had been.

"I'm ready," she told him firmly.

The roomy 747 was a beehive of activity as passengers stowed their belongings and fastened their seat belts. One of the stewardesses approached with a professionally cheerful smile that became genuine when it was turned on Josh.

"Can I get you something to drink after take-off?" she asked.

When Sabrina declined, Josh's eyes narrowed on her strained face. "It's been a rather hectic day. I think a drink might relax you."

Perhaps he was right. "Bring me . . . I don't know. What shall I have?" she asked vaguely.

"My wife will have a glass of champagne," he told the stewardess. The look he gave Sabrina was full of mischief. "It's better not to mix your drinks." His voice dropped to a husky murmur as he added, "At least not here."

Swift color stained her pale cheeks. She knew Josh was

alluding to a party where their host had urged her to sample some rare brandy after she had been drinking wine. Since Sabrina wasn't normally much of a drinker, the effect was disastrous. Josh had carried her into the bedroom when they got home, crooning comforting things as he undressed her. When he held her pliant body against him so he could remove her panties, Sabrina's head began spinning for a different reason.

In the end she had begged for his possession, begged for release from the exquisite torment of his hands and lips on her body.

As Sabrina relived that night of passion, her heart started to thunder so loudly that it rivaled the roaring engines of the plane. Her long lashes made feathery fans on her flushed cheeks. From the flame in Josh's amber eyes, she knew he was remembering that night too.

Sabrina caught her breath, turning toward the window. That was all over with, the part of the marriage that was based on illusion and lies. At least this one would be straightforward—as long as it lasted.

The plane gained altitude, leaving Los Angeles behind. Somewhere in the sprawling metropolis was the opulent oasis of Beverly Hills, sanctuary of the rich and powerful. Sabrina had been so sure she had left it forever when she finally struck out on her own. Now she would be returning to that fool's paradise, knowing it for what it was this time. How long until she was free once more? How long until she could be sure her actions wouldn't jeopardize Simon's precarious health?

As if he could read her thoughts, Josh commented dryly. "Well, at least we left a happy man behind."

"I still don't see why he insisted we go to Europe. In fact, I'm amazed that he would let you go *anywhere* while he's laid up in the hospital." Josh was second in command

13

at the conglomerate her grandfather headed. Sabrina quirked a sardonic eyebrow. "Who's watching the store?"

"I'm grooming Tom Edderley for more responsibility," Josh replied. "This will be a good chance for him to get his feet wet—see if he can handle things."

Sabrina smiled. "You sounded just like Simon then."

"I'd be proud to be half the man he is. Simon was a great teacher."

"And you were an attentive pupil," she responded wryly.

Josh had come to Ameropol right out of Harvard Business School fifteen years earlier. In spite of his youth he had risen rapidly in the ranks, becoming something of a legend in the business world. Through the years Josh had many offers to head other corporations, but he remained loyal to Simon, who regarded him almost as a son. Perhaps because his relations with his own son had been less than perfect.

"It helps when you're interested in the subject," Josh answered her observation.

Sabrina knew that he was more than interested. Josh had a goal. "It must be nice to know what you want out of life."

His eyes glowed with sudden intensity as they rested on her delicate features. "Yes, I've always known exactly what I wanted."

She didn't pretend to misunderstand. "Too bad it wasn't enough for you when you got it!" Sabrina uttered bitterly, before she could stop herself. She bit her lip, turning her head away. "I'm sorry, Josh, I shouldn't have said that. It's stupid to dwell on the past."

His hand cupped her chin, gently guiding her to face him. She trembled from the contact, feeling the warmth of his body subtly seducing her. Josh's low voice was like liquid honey. "I think about it constantly. All the way

14

back to the time you came to live with Simon. You were beautiful even then."

Sabrina smiled unwillingly. "What a convenient memory you have. I was skinny, and shy, and my hair was always in my eyes." Her sudden laughter was completely natural. "Remember the time I got bubble gum in it and cut it all off? Grandfather was furious."

"And you came running to me because you were terrified." Josh's eyes were soft with remembrance. "Didn't you know he wouldn't lay a finger on you?"

"I honestly didn't at the time. He got angry with me so seldom."

"And you had to live with the mistake so long," Josh recalled. "It took months to grow out."

"You didn't have to laugh at me," she protested. "That hurt more than Simon's hollering."

"Did it, Sabrina?" His long fingers caressed her neck, slipping sensuously through the soft, silky hair. "Why?"

She jerked away as a shiver went down her spine. "You know perfectly well that I had a crush on you. All my friends did. We used to speculate about what you looked like without your clothes."

Josh gave a shout of laughter. "You little devils!"

She returned his grin. "Men can't claim to have a corner on that sort of thing."

"I can't promise to have noticed you were a woman at thirteen, but by sixteen I was having trouble restraining myself. I think I deserve a medal for patience."

After a quick glance, Sabrina looked away. Was Josh referring to their first real date, the one that was the start of everything?

She had been throwing herself at him for years, but Josh had refused to take her seriously, pretending it was a joke. He watched indulgently as she went out first with high-school boys, and later college men, always hoping it would make him jealous. She had almost given up hope when soon after her nineteenth birthday, Josh made his move. He took her dinner dancing. It was the most perfect night of her life. When he held her in his arms, resting his lips on her temple, Sabrina thought she would surely die of happiness. But, she recalled bitterly, Josh was simply making the opening gambit in his game plan.

On the way home he had asked if she minded stopping at his house for some reports Simon wanted dropped off. Sabrina was delighted with anything that would prolong the evening. While Josh shuffled through the papers on his desk, she gazed around the comfortable den. It was a beautiful room, it had been a beautiful evening—the whole world was beautiful! In an excess of pure joy, Sabrina threw her arms around Josh, pressing her soft lips against the strong column of his neck.

After a startled moment, his arms closed convulsively around her. When she lifted an eager face, his mouth reached hungrily for hers, plundering the moist recess with a male aggression that started a fire in her veins. Sabrina unbuttoned his shirt instinctively, sliding her hands inside to glide over his hair-roughened chest. With a low groan, he captured her fingers, but then she rained kisses on his bronze skin.

"Sabrina, for God's sake stop it," he begged. "You don't know what you're doing to me!"

"Make love to me, Josh," she murmured, molding her body the length of his.

He shook her hard. "Are you out of your mind?" he demanded harshly.

Sabrina's passion-glazed eyes suddenly focused. Her blood chilled as she realized that she had thrown herself at Josh and had been rejected. Shame washed over her in a choking wave. She turned her back, unable to face him.

Josh drew her flinching body against him, wrapping his

16

arms around her and burying his face in her scented hair. "It's all right, darling. It was my fault for bringing you here. I underestimated my self-control."

"You don't have to be kind," she mumbled through her tears. "We both know I made a fool of myself."

He had nuzzled the silky hair aside so he could blow softly in her ear. "You could never do that, sweetheart."

The tears flowed faster. "Please don't, Josh. I know how you feel about me."

"Do you really?" He turned her in his arms, his eyes blazing with a scorching light. "Do you know that it's all I can do right now to keep from carrying you into the bedroom and undressing you so I can touch every inch of that beautiful body?"

Sabrina's breath caught in her throat. "You . . . you want to make love to me?"

"Every night of my life." His fingertips traced an erotic pattern over her shoulders, dipping down to the shadowed valley between her breasts. "I want to marry you. But not yet," he added firmly, holding her away when she would have rushed into his arms. "You're too young yet, and I won't take advantage of it."

Sabrina tried in vain that night to persuade him, but Josh couldn't hold out for long. They were married three months later. How long was it until he took up with his girlfriend again? Sabrina wondered bitterly. Or hadn't they ever stopped seeing each other? His infidelity after only eight months of marriage opened Sabrina's eyes. If he had merely tired of her, she might even have understood. Her rank inexperience couldn't compete with the sophisticated women he had known. But Josh kept up the fiction of undying love, in a desperate attempt to prevent her from leaving him. That was when Sabrina realized she was Josh's passport to power. He was willing to pay any price to reach his goal.

17

Josh broke the little silence that had grown between them. "Do you realize this is the first chance we've had to talk? All those hours in the hospital were devoted solely to Simon."

Sabrina gave him a little smile. "He does have a way of dominating the scene."

"I don't even know what you've been doing with yourself since you moved to New York."

She looked up quickly, suspecting a putdown. Sabrina was very sensitive about her former dependency. She had been raised as a social butterfly without any marketable skills. It made her present independence doubly sweet. She had taken nothing from either Josh or Simon—and she had survived. She wasn't about to put up with his doubting her independence now.

"I'm a translator at the United Nations," she finally replied. Her fluency in languages had been her salvation.

"Good for you!"

Sabrina glowed with pride at the respect in his eyes. "I hope I can get my job back when we . . . when I . . ." She floundered to a halt.

Josh's face hardened. "Isn't that rather negative thinking?"

"I don't see why. It's just realistic." She caught her lower lip between her small white teeth. "We both know this marriage is a formality, something we did for Simon's sake."

"Are you sure, Sabrina?"

Her startled eyes flew to his face. "I told you the only way I'd go through with it was if you agreed not . . . if there was no . . ."

"No lovemaking?" His mouth curved in a cruel smile. "Tell me, Sabrina, how many men have you had since you left me?"

18

"None!" She gasped. "Not that it's any of your business."

His hand circled her neck, the thumb idly rotating over the rapidly beating pulse at the base of her throat as he ignored the stern tone in her voice. His eyes were cynical as he watched the pink tide flood her translucent skin. "Poor baby. You must have missed me."

"I didn't," she denied stiffly.

Josh chuckled softly. "You couldn't have changed that completely, Sabrina. I'm the man you were married to, remember?"

"That doesn't mean you know everything about me."

"I know how to please you." His low voice was seductive. "We learned it together, didn't we?"

Sabrina felt like a small, trapped animal. If only she could get away, be alone to think. Her body was arched rigidly against the confining seat belt. "That's part of the past. I don't think about it any more."

"Do you really expect me to believe that?" he asked lazily. Josh's hand went to the small of her back, massaging the tense muscles. His fingers slowly teased their way up her spine. "You're a beautiful, passionate woman, my dear. I don't think you can live without love."

"You're talking about sex, not love!"

"All right, let's talk about sex." His hand brushed lightly over her rib cage, tantalizingly close to the soft swell of her breast. "We've always been good together— and we *are* legally married. What's wrong with making the best of our bargain?"

She grabbed for his disruptive hand, flinging it back at him violently. "You're disgusting! Just the sound of that makes me feel cheap."

Josh eyed her flushed cheeks thoughtfully. "We're going to be together for two weeks, day and night. Feeling the way we do about each other, it could be quite a strain."

"I don't feel *any* way about you!" she flared, aware that they were beginning to attract the attention of several nearby passengers.

"Silly little Sabrina," he murmured, bending his dark head to her bright one.

Before she could turn her face away, his hand was on her cheek, holding her for a kiss that was devastating. Josh's lips moved over hers so lightly that she could barely feel them, but when his warm tongue traced the outline of her tightly closed mouth, Sabrina drew in her breath sharply. It afforded him the access he wanted, and he kissed her openly, possessively.

Josh's breathing was ragged as he lifted his head. He framed her face in his palms, running his fingers through her long, pale hair. "Sabrina, my darling," he murmured huskily. "How can you deny we were meant for each other?"

As she gazed up at him mutely, melting in the topaz glow of his eyes, a distraction brought her back to her senses. A stewardess was standing over them.

"Excuse me," the attendant said brightly. "Can I put your tray tables down? We're going to be serving dinner shortly."

"I won't ever forgive you for this," Sabrina hissed when the stewardess had gone. "How could you embarrass me like that?"

"I imagine she's seen two people kissing before." Josh's grin was unrepentant. "It isn't as though we were doing what we'd like to have been doing."

Sabrina sat back in her seat, composing herself with effort. "You know, you're partially right, Josh. You're a wonderful lover, and my body remembers. You make me come alive so easily." She forced the next words through trembling lips. "But the only thing left between us is sex, and that's not enough. I don't love you any more."

Sabrina waited breathlessly to see if he would believe the lie. He simply *had* to! She was independent now, finally a person in her own right. But Josh could destroy all that if he knew she loved him. He could bind her to him with invisible chains as strong as real ones, he could begin to use her again. She would never escape, and that would be the ultimate disaster. One-sided love brought only misery to the one cursed to do the loving.

Josh studied her tormented face for a long moment. Then he lifted her hand and kissed the palm. "Put your doubts to rest, love. I'll stick to the agreement." He gave her a teasing smile. "I'll take a lot of cold showers."

"It won't work, Josh, I—"

"Listen to me, Sabrina," he interrupted. "We've always had a lot of fun together—in and out of bed." He just couldn't resist adding that with a grin. "Why let a little thing like marriage spoil a long friendship? We'll go sightseeing and poke around in fun little shops, just generally unwind. I, for one, can use a vacation. How about it?"

"I just don't think it's a good idea," she answered helplessly.

"Why not?" he asked casually. "Now that I know it's really over between us, I won't bother you any more." There was a stillness about him as he waited for her answer.

"Well, I—I suppose if I don't go through with this 'honeymoon,' it would be kind of awkward, explaining it to Simon, I mean."

"That's true. We're doing all this for him in the first place." Josh's face lit up as he greeted the stewardess. "Ah, here's our dinner."

Sabrina nibbled her food absently. She should have been happy that Josh accepted her conditions so readily, but her heart shriveled up inside her. He could only have done that if it didn't matter one way or the other. Well, at least that meant he would keep his promise. Sabrina knew she could never hold out against him if he made a concerted effort to seduce her in the privacy of their hotel room.

Josh looked over at her tray, still nearly full. "Eat your dinner, love. You're going to need your strength." He gave her a melting smile. "This is one honeymoon we're both going to remember for the rest of our lives."

CHAPTER TWO

Once Sabrina and Josh checked into the hotel in Amsterdam, the manager followed the European custom of escorting them to their room. It turned out to be the bridal suite. He was very obsequious, assuring them that even without the trans-Atlantic phone call from Simon's personal secretary, the management would have spared no effort to accommodate the granddaughter of Simon Sheffield—and of course her husband.

He showed them through the beautiful suite, pointing with pride to the lovely antiques and graceful breakfront filled with beautifully illustrated books on painting and sculpture. Sabrina couldn't give the sitting room that much attention because her mind was on the bedroom. There was only one. She slanted a panicky look at Josh, but for once he was no help. He wore a nonplussed look of his own.

Oblivious to their discomfort, the manager led them into the bedroom where he gestured grandly toward the magnificent view of the river and the city beyond.

Josh cleared his throat. "It's very nice, but isn't the . . . er . . . bed a little small?"

The manager smiled deprecatingly. "Ah yes, Americans are used to—what do you call them?—king-sized beds. We in Europe still favor the double bed." He regarded it fondly. "This is a particularly fine example of the Louis Seize period."

What difference did it make? Sabrina quietly signaled her feelings to Josh. She wasn't going to share the bed with him no matter what size it was. When he didn't ask for different accommodations, she started to do it herself.

Josh cut her off neatly. Easing the man out the door, he assured him that they were delighted with the suite and everything in it.

When they were alone, Sabrina turned on Josh like a virago. "Why didn't you tell him we needed two rooms? How could you let him walk out thinking we were going to stay?" Her eyes were like flashing emeralds. "I must have been out of my mind to trust you for one second, Joshua Winchester! I'll bet you knew about this all along."

His hands were firm on her slim shoulders, remaining there when she tried to shrug them off. "Calm down and listen to me, Sabrina. I had nothing to do with this. Simon's office made all the arrangements."

"So what? You could have told him this was very nice but we prefer separate rooms."

"Did you hear what he said? Simon's secretary made the reservations personally. If I know Hilda, she's going to call back to find out if the champagne was delivered on time and if there are enough towels in the bathroom." He ran his fingers through his thick, dark hair. "She's a fantastic secretary, but she boxed us in neatly this time."

"I don't see why. When she calls, we'll just say everything is dandy. We don't have to tell her we switched rooms."

"She won't call *us*. Hilda would never bother us on our honeymoon. She'll call the manager—like a drill sergeant checking up on the troops."

"Oh." Sabrina quickly rallied her defenses. "What difference does it make if she finds out? We don't have to explain our sleeping arrangements to Simon's secretary."

Josh raised a sardonic eyebrow. "How about to Simon? Your grandfather planned this honeymoon, and he's living it vicariously. He's going to expect bulletins from Hilda at every stop. If we move out of the honeymoon suite at our very first hotel, what do you imagine he's going to think?"

The logic of Josh's reasoning made Sabrina bite her lower lip. "But, Josh, what are we going to do?"

"Make the best of it." He shrugged, glancing around the elegant sitting room. "I'll sleep on the couch."

The sofa was French, like the rest of the furnishings. Its scaled-down, curved shape was covered in satin damask, deeply tufted all over with small buttons.

"You can't possibly," Sabrina stated flatly. "Even if you weren't a foot longer than that thing, you'd get curvature of the spine trying to fit yourself to it."

Josh laughed. "Only over a long period. Hopefully, the next hotel will have decent-sized furniture."

"Oh, Josh." Her face was dismayed. "I can't ask you to do that for two weeks. This is your vacation—the first real one you've had in years. Can't you think of an alternative?"

"Well, I guess I could rent a room down the street," he teased. "That would be a switch, wouldn't it? A man sneaking *out* of a beautiful woman's room."

She refused to smile, her soft mouth drooping disconsolately. "I knew we shouldn't have let Simon talk us into this."

Josh put his arm around her. "You're tired, honey. It's been a long trip. Why don't you go in and take a nap? Everything's going to work out, I promise you."

"You must be tired too." She eyed the couch doubtfully.

"I'll be fine." He gave her a gentle push.

Just as she started for the bedroom, the phone rang un-

25

expectedly. Sabrina's surprise was followed by apprehension. Did Simon have another relapse? She let Josh answer, relaxing when she realized he was talking to a friend.

As she again began to leave the room, Josh motioned her back to him, putting his arm around her waist as he talked animatedly. It was such a natural, affectionate act that her heart twisted. They might almost be married—*really* married. She put her arm tentatively around his lean torso, feeling the shifting muscles. The warmth of his body invaded hers, running through her in a hot tide as his tactile fingers made absentminded, but erotic, circles over her stomach.

"Wha . . . what?" She was aware that Josh had asked her something.

He had his hand over the mouthpiece. "I said Hans Hallen is having a party tonight. Do you feel up to going?"

"Oh . . . I—I suppose so."

Josh frowned at her bemused face. "I'd better tell him we can't make it."

"No, I'm okay." She pulled herself together, carefully moving out of his embrace. "I don't know him, but a party sounds like fun."

After Josh hung up, he shook his head ruefully. "That grandfather of yours is something else. When he insisted we go to Europe on our honeymoon, I should have suspected he had more than romance on his mind."

"What do you mean?"

"Hans Hallen consolidates our mining interests over here, and Simon just happened to give him a call, telling him I'd be arriving today. He also suggested that if Hans got the tonnage figures together for all the northern countries, I'd be able to go over them with him."

"That's terrible!" Sabrina declared indignantly, before the humor of it struck her. "I wouldn't put it past Grandfather to write this trip off as a business expense."

Josh's eyes brimmed with merriment. "Can you doubt it?"

"Well, this is one time he won't get away with it. We won't go to the party if it's going to be all business."

"No, it's purely social, and I think we should go. Hans is a good fellow; you'll enjoy yourself."

"All right, but if he tries to back you into a corner, I'm going to carry you off," she warned.

"I'd like that," Josh said softly. When she looked doubtfully at the sudden glint in his eyes, he turned her toward the bedroom. "If we're going out tonight you'd definitely better take a nap. No matter what time it is here, it's the middle of the night for us."

After Sabrina undressed and got into bed, she realized how tired she was. It wasn't just the difference in time, it was the traumatic events of the last twenty-four hours. Could she and Josh survive the next two weeks without something dire happening? Sabrina turned restlessly under the down duvet, her body aching from more than weariness.

It was dark when she awoke. Sabrina stretched luxuriously, sliding out of bed and shivering slightly as the cool air chilled her sleep warm body. She had slept in just a pair of lace bikini panties because she was too tired to unpack. She opened her suitcases now, rummaging for her negligee, a frothy concoction of lavender chiffon and satin ribbons. But once she found it and considered its transparency, she reluctantly put it aside, choosing instead her satin robe.

Sabrina looked at her watch, frowning. How much time did she have to get ready? Josh hadn't mentioned when they were due at the party.

She opened the bedroom door softly in case he was still sleeping—then she froze with fright. Josh was lying flat on the floor next to the couch.

She ran to him, sinking down on her knees and lifting

27

his head into her lap. "Josh, what happened? Are you all right?" She brushed the dark hair off his forehead, bending down to search his face hopefully. "Please be all right, darling."

He opened his eyes slowly, like a sleepy lion. The slightly puzzled expression changed swiftly as he gazed into Sabrina's face just inches from his. "If this is a dream, don't bother to wake me for a week or two."

"Did you fall?" Her fingertips made fluttery motions over his face and shoulders. "Are you hurt?"

His hand curved around the back of her neck, urging her gently closer. "If I am, will you kiss it and make it better?"

Sabrina sat back on her heels sharply. "There's nothing wrong with you. What are you doing on the floor?"

He sat up, wincing slightly. "Sleeping. You were right, that couch is shaped for a stooped midget."

"I *told* you so," she remarked in exasperation. "Why didn't you come to me and admit it?"

"What would that have accomplished?" His tawny eyes traveled slowly down her body. "Unless you've changed your mind about sharing the bedroom."

"Certainly not!" She hurriedly wrapped her robe more tightly around her. "I would have switched with you. That's what I should have suggested in the first place."

"Do you think I want a bride who looks like a semicolon?"

"It's the only solution, Josh. You can't go on sleeping on the floor."

"We'll talk about it later, honey. Right now we'd better get ready." He pulled the shirt out of his slacks and started unbuttoning it. "You can take the first shower—unless you want to take it together," he teased.

"You never give up, do you?" she said with a sigh.

"Not where you're concerned," he answered softly.

Was that a warning? In the muted light from the open bedroom door Josh gave the impression of a virile animal ready to spring. The diffused glow cast shadows on his lean face, making his eyes gleam deviously.

Sabrina drew a deep breath, banishing the fantasy. "I'll go take my shower."

As she started to get up, Josh caught her wrist. "Were you really worried about me?"

"Well, of course I was."

"Why, Sabrina?"

"That's a foolish question."

"Did I hear you call me darling?" His fingers slid up her arm, the back of his hand touching her breast.

She reacted like she'd been scalded, jerking away. "Don't be ridiculous! Why would I do that? And please let me go or I'll never be ready in time."

He didn't stop her this time, watching her hurried departure with enigmatic eyes.

After they were both dressed Sabrina felt more comfortable. Not that Josh wasn't just as dangerous with his clothes on, she reflected grimly. It just made Sabrina feel more secure about resisting him.

The gown she had chosen was a pale-yellow silk with a low-draped neckline that molded her small, high breasts. The color blended with her creamy skin and golden hair.

Josh stood behind her, appraising Sabrina in the mirror. "Mmm, very nice, but it needs something." He drew a long velvet box out of his pocket.

She looked at him blankly. "What's this?"

"Open it and see," he smiled.

On a bed of satin was a sparkling circlet of diamonds, contoured to fit around the base of her slender throat. Sabrina gasped. "For me?"

"Well, they certainly aren't for me," he replied.

"But I can't accept this!"

29

"It's my wedding present." His eyes held hers steadily. "I thought you'd like it better than emeralds."

Sabrina's long lashes fell, remembering his first wedding present to her, a beautiful emerald bracelet. She hadn't taken it with her when she left Josh's house. "We were married such a short time . . ." Her words trailed off.

"Was that it, Sabrina? Or didn't you want anything that would remind you of me?" She looked up swiftly at the odd note in his voice, finding an indecipherable expression. "Well, never mind."

He slipped the blazing circlet around her slender neck. Josh's long fingers sent a shiver down her back as he fastened the intricate clasp. Putting his hands on her shoulders, he regarded her in the mirror with satisfaction, his tanned face and dark hair a stunning contrast to her blond features.

The string of diamonds twinkled like individual stars, their hard brilliance emphasizing the softness of her flawless skin. Sabrina touched the necklace with a tentative forefinger. "It's beautiful, Josh."

His hands tightened on her shoulders. "On you it is."

"But it must have cost a fortune," she protested weakly.

He folded his arms over her breasts, burying his face in the perfumed cloud of her hair. "You're worth it, my precious golden girl."

Sabrina stiffened, the hot tide of blood cooling. What a fool she was to think his lavish gift was an expression of love. Actually, it was simply an investment. Josh had plenty of money. Through the years, Simon had rewarded his brilliance with bonuses and stock options. Josh was independently wealthy, but it wasn't enough for him. It was power he was after. When you have everything else at thirty-six, what is left?

Sabrina's burning anger was fed by disappointment and

a desolation she refused to admit to herself. Moving out of his arms, she said coolly, "Not yet I'm not."

Josh misunderstood—or pretended to misunderstand. "Are you saying you'll have to perform well in bed to merit having the necklace?"

"You know that's not what I meant!" She turned away, fumbling with the clasp.

His hands closed over her shaking fingers, cupping the back of her neck. "Why are you making such a big deal out of this?" he demanded.

Sabrina's anger flared out of control as she glared up at him. "Because I won't be bought like a stock issue—or one of your other investments!"

He ran his hand through his thick sable hair. "What the hell is that supposed to mean?"

If Sabrina hadn't known better, she might almost have believed his air of puzzlement. "Oh, forget it! Just take this thing back."

He jerked her wrists down to her sides, holding them in a viselike grip. Josh was suddenly blazing with as much anger as Sabrina. "It's yours. Do whatever you want with it. As far as I'm concerned you can throw the damn thing in the river!"

He strode out of the room, leaving Sabrina speechless and confused. Had she misinterpreted his intentions? One thing was certain, she couldn't leave the valuable necklace in the suite. Her soft mouth set in a straight line. Well, what difference did it make if she wore it tonight? It was all part of the sham of their forced marriage. It could join the emerald bracelet in the drawer when she would leave Josh for the second time.

Catching up a white mink jacket and a small gold evening purse, Sabrina entered the sitting room with her head held high. "I'm ready," she said confidently.

He helped her into her coat without comment, standing

31

back politely to let her precede him out the door. They walked to the elevator in a heavy silence that continued in the car Josh had hired for the duration of their stay. Sabrina tried in vain to think of something neutral to say. They couldn't go through a whole evening like this. But from Josh's grim profile, he had every intention of doing just that.

When they reached the party, however, he slipped back into his sophisticated, urbane role. No one would have suspected he was anything but a devoted husband.

Hans Hallen's apartment was in a tall building facing the river. High windows draped in tasseled damask looked out on a striking view of the charming old city. The expansive living room was filled with well-dressed people, none of whom Sabrina knew.

"So, I finally have the pleasure of meeting your beautiful wife." Her host's huge hand engulfed Sabrina's small one.

She glanced up at a blond giant, liking his rugged, open countenance immediately. His tall wife was equally gracious. After introductions had been exchanged, Rena Hallen said, "We were delighted to hear that you had accompanied Josh this trip. I was very disappointed that he did not bring you in March."

That was three months ago! Didn't they know she and Josh had been divorced? When their hosts turned to greet other guests, Sabrina murmured to Josh, "You didn't tell them?"

He shrugged. "There didn't seem any reason to. It wasn't really important."

Sabrina paled as though he had slapped her. Why did it hurt so much when she'd known it all along?

Josh relented when he saw the expression on her face. "I mean, they'd never met you."

"You don't have to explain. I understand," she answered stiffly.

32

He stared at her for a long moment, an inexplicable look in his hooded eyes. "I wonder if you ever have," he said softly.

Their hostess rejoined them, leading Sabrina into the long room to introduce her to the other guests. To Sabrina's surprise, Josh trailed along. She would have thought he'd accept the respite from her company gratefully. Then she realized he was only keeping up appearances.

Sabrina exchanged pleasantries with the others, her smile never betraying her aching awareness of the sardonic man beside her. Especially when she was forced to acknowledge compliments.

"This husband of yours is so fascinating," an older woman informed her. "I wonder that you allow him to travel without you."

"Sabrina trusts me implicitly," Josh answered for her, a bland look on his face. "Why would a man look at another woman when he has a wife as sweet and gentle as mine?"

Sabrina bristled at the underlying mockery. "Who is also the granddaughter of your boss," she added sweetly. "Don't forget that."

He put his arm around her waist in a show of affection as the group around them laughed, thinking their teasing was innocent. "With your attributes I would have been tempted to marry you anyway, my love."

Before Sabrina could think of a way to retaliate, another couple joined them.

"I've been admiring your necklace all the way across the room," the woman said. She was youthful and attractive. "It's positively smashing."

"Thank you," Sabrina replied, avoiding Josh's eyes.

The woman aimed a provocative glance at her husband. "I hope it give you ideas for my birthday next month."

The man sighed dramatically. "Josh is determined to

33

ruin the rest of us. I'll go bankrupt trying to keep up with him."

"Don't look at it that way," Josh advised smoothly. "Think of all the fringe benefits accrued, the little cries of delight, the words of gratitude. I can't tell you all the things Sabrina said to me when I presented her with the necklace."

Sabrina's green eyes slanted angrily. She slid her arm through Josh's, unconsciously digging her nails into the rich fabric of his coat sleeve. "And I'm not through yet. Just wait till you hear what I have to say to you later."

Josh's derisive smile acknowledged that the game was no longer one-sided.

A few minutes later, someone claimed his attention and Sabrina was free at last. She couldn't stand this charade one more second! This cold thrust and parry, with no objective except to wound, made her faintly ill. What had happened to all the caring?

Taking refuge in the darkened den, Sabrina leaned her forehead against the glass pane of the window. Closing her eyes to hold back the tears, she sagged under the weight of the misery washing over her. A sound startled her, like a frightened animal when it hears the hunter approaching.

"Sabrina?" As she stiffened defensively, a look of pain crossed Josh's face. "I'm sorry." His deep voice was muted. "I behaved abominably."

She searched his face warily, expecting a trick. "Yes, you did. It wasn't very fair of you when I couldn't fight back."

The smile he gave her was rueful. "I'd say you gave as good as you got." Then, when he saw her anger beginning to flare, he quickly continued. "I really did come to apologize. Will you forgive me?" Sabrina hesitated, and he took her cold hands. "If I promise never to buy you anything again?" Josh teased, trying to ease the terrible strain on her face.

She snatched her hands away. "You know that's not what the argument was about!"

He rumpled his thick hair in bafflement. "I honestly don't understand what brought on this whole thing. All I know is that I can't stand hurting you. I want to make you happy, not miserable."

Sabrina felt the familiar melting of her resistance. Josh could charm a charging elephant. She hardened her heart, refusing to let him use his wiles on her. "You haven't done a very good job of it," she told him coldly.

"There's one way I know of to make you happy," he said. "But you won't let me use that." His fingers trailed across her cheek to trace the shape of her trembling lips.

She retreated until her back was against the window. "There has to be more than that, Josh."

"There is, sweetheart." He followed her, his hands spanning her narrow waist, urging her toward him. "There's friendship and laughter, a million memories of happy times."

But no mention of love, she thought dully. When Josh's hands traced the curved shape of her hips, Sabrina grabbed for them, throwing them off her. "No, Josh! I won't let you do this to me again."

"I don't intend to, love—not ever."

He thought she meant quarreling in public. He didn't realize she was afraid of something far more devastating. Josh had once enslaved her, body and soul. He must never be allowed to do it again.

Suddenly he reached out and swept her into a hard embrace, cradling her head on his shoulder. "I want so badly to make you happy. You don't know how much I've missed you. That's the reason I didn't tell the Hallens we were divorced; so I could talk about you and pretend you were waiting for me at home."

Sabrina could feel the familiar magic engulfing her. Josh

35

held her so tightly that she was molded to the full length of him, his hard thighs thrusting against hers. The steady beat of his heart seemed to enter her own breast making them one person.

She struggled not to succumb, not to let his lean body arouse the hunger for him that had never gone away. "You said I wasn't important," she muttered.

"No, my love, that's not what I said." He cupped her chin in his hand, raising her face to his. In the filtered moonlight shining through the window, his eyes had a molten gleam. "Don't you know you're the most important thing in my life?"

His mouth closed over hers in a kiss that was almost ruthless. Josh was putting his brand of possession on her, serving notice that he would never let her go. Sabrina's brain sounded a warning that her body refused to heed. Josh's tongue was a torch, lighting a flame that traveled like wildfire. His hands fanned the blaze, slipping inside the low neck of her gown to caress her breast lingeringly. When he pressed her lower body against him, a shudder swept Sabrina. With a soft sigh of surrender, she wound her arms around his neck, straining against him and returning the kiss with a passion that rivaled his.

They were oblivious to their surroundings, lost in an exquisite world of sensation. It came as a shock when a bright light intruded on their privacy.

"Oh, I—I'm terribly sorry." Hans looked embarrassed. "I didn't know . . . that is, I came to get . . ."

Sabrina's embarrassment was as acute as their host's, yet Josh's only emotion was annoyance, which he managed to control. "I suppose we're the ones who should apologize for leaving the party, but we're on our honeymoon . . . still," he added.

The huge blond man grinned. "I will understand perfectly if you do not stay for supper."

"Wouldn't think of leaving," Josh replied cheerfully. He kissed the top of Sabrina's head. "I'm going to need plenty of sustenance."

"Josh!" She gasped.

He laughed, one arm tightening around her shoulders. "Come on, honey, you must be starved. We haven't had anything to eat since the plane ride."

"Splendid." Hans beamed. "The buffet is being prepared now."

Sabrina suddenly realized that Josh was right, she was hungry. A little annoyance lingered at the way he had embarrassed her, yet she couldn't regret their reconciliation. Maybe everything he said was a lie, but that kiss had told the truth. Physically, they were like matches and dynamite. Josh might not love her, but his desire for her was still potent. It was both a danger and a small comfort.

For the first time, Sabrina started to enjoy the party. Josh was effortlessly charming most of the time, so when he exerted himself as he did during dinner, he was irresistible. Sabrina found herself laughing and talking easily, all tension drained away.

After the delicious buffet though, she was conscious of being tired again. The difference in time between continents was confusing to sleep patterns the first day of a trip. Sabrina was having trouble stifling her yawns.

With Josh's uncanny ability to sense her every emotion, he was instantly aware of her fatigue. Thinking he might want to stay longer, Sabrina assured him that she felt fine, but Josh insisted on leaving.

They were relaxed in the car driving back to the hotel, making plans for the next day. It wasn't until they entered the suite that the unsolved problem of their sleeping arrangements occurred to Sabrina. She immediately broached the solution of her sleeping on the sofa, which Josh refused to consider.

37

"You promised to take me to Keukenhoff Gardens tomorrow," she pointed out. "How are you going to do that if you're out on your feet?"

"I'll be in good shape," he insisted. "I never did need much sleep."

"There's a big difference between not much and none," she answered tartly. "There *must* be some solution." Her smooth brow wrinkled. "Wasn't there a classic movie about this once?"

"Not exactly. Clark Gable hung a sheet between twin beds to preserve Claudette Colbert's virtue. But if we had twin beds we wouldn't be in this predicament."

"I suppose you're right." Sabrina sighed heavily.

Josh laughed. "Cheer up, sweetheart. If nothing else, I'm proving that chivalry isn't dead."

She watched indecisively as he pulled back the spread to get a pillow. When he started toward the door with it, Sabrina made up her mind.

"This is ridiculous! We're acting like children. There's no reason why we can't share the bed together."

"You thought of several when I suggested that myself," Josh observed dryly.

"You know very well we're not talking about the same thing! It's just the only solution to a bad situation. Under the circumstances I'm sure I can trust you not to take any unfair advantage."

Josh didn't look as convinced. "You're asking a lot of a mere mortal."

"Work at it," she advised callously. "Thinking about the alternative ought to dampen your ardor."

Sabrina was purposely matter-of-fact because she was having her own doubts. It was going to be torture to sleep in the same bed with Josh—a bed so small that she'd be able to feel the actual heat of his body. The main thing to guard against was any physical contact. The mere thought

38

of it caused a tingling sensation deep within her. But what other solution was there? Josh simply couldn't sleep on the floor for nights on end.

He sighed, removing his tie and starting to unbutton his shirt. "You drive a hard bargain, Mrs. Winchester."

As he completed the job, shrugging the shirt off his muscled torso, Sabrina was swept by a flood of memories. A vivid picture arose of the way they used to go to sleep in each other's arms, waking the next morning in almost the same position.

Josh was unbuckling his belt. Did he intend to get undressed right there in front of her? With an inarticulate little sound deep in her throat, she caught up her nightgown and robe, fleeing into the bathroom.

After giving him plenty of time to undress and get into bed, Sabrina hesitantly appeared in the doorway. Josh's shoulders were bare above the covers, and she wondered fleetingly if he still slept in the nude. It didn't bear thinking about.

"You . . . uh . . . you can turn out the lights," she murmured.

The lamp was still lit, making Sabrina self-consciously aware of how sheer her filmy gown was beneath her robe. Especially since Josh was inspecting her with lively male interest.

"I didn't want you to stumble in the dark." He watched her rapid progress across the room with hidden amusement.

She removed her robe quickly, feeling Josh's eyes on her shoulders and breasts like a tangible caress. Scrambling into bed, Sabrina pulled the covers up to her chin with a sigh of relief.

"Does that flimsy little scrap keep you warm?" he asked conversationally.

As warm as *I* used to? was the implicit question. "Warm enough," she answered curtly.

"You used to hate nightgowns," he persisted. "You said they got all tangled up during the night."

"I've changed."

"So you keep telling me," he murmured cynically.

"Go to sleep, Josh," she ordered sharply.

Her heart started to hammer as he levered himself up in bed, leaning over to turn her face toward him. In the darkness his features were indistinct, but the long fingers stroking her cheek were very, very real. Sabrina could scarcely breathe as his mouth touched hers. She parted her lips automatically, but Josh didn't deepen the kiss.

"Good night, my love," he said huskily.

Sabrina stared into the darkness, holding herself rigidly to control the emotion racing through her. It was torture to have him this close. One touch from Josh could destroy all her noble resolve. It was a good thing he didn't know it. If his hand had trailed down her aching body, touching her as only he knew how . . . Sabrina squeezed her eyes tightly shut to obliterate the tantalizing image.

CHAPTER THREE

Sabrina turned restlessly in her sleep. She was usually a very quiet sleeper, but a subtle awareness of something different disturbed her.

She sighed and flung one arm out, encountering a firm yet yielding, warm presence. Moving closer to the middle of the bed, Sabrina settled her head on Josh's shoulder with a tiny sigh of contentment, her arm curving around his neck.

He remained very still for a long moment, drinking in the perfume of her skin. Then he gently tried to disentangle the arm that tightened stubbornly. As Josh was guiding her back to her own side of the bed, Sabrina's eyes opened.

For a moment she was confused. Josh's hands on her shoulders were a remembered blessing. She waited for them to continue down her receptive body, an inarticulate little sound of satisfaction escaping from her parted lips.

He groaned deeply, his hands tightening on her shoulders to push her back against the pillows. "Wake up, Sabrina," he ordered harshly.

She took his unwilling hand, drawing it down to her breast; it cupped her convulsively. "I am awake," she murmured.

His fingers found her nipple, circling it lingeringly, as if he couldn't help himself. Tiny shock waves ran through her at the familiar male touch that always turned her liq-

41

uid inside. When he started to remove his hand she caught his wrist, guiding his fingers to her other breast.

"Stop it, Sabrina! You don't know what you're doing."

Perhaps she hadn't at first. In the velvety darkness she had sought Josh instinctively, her subconscious knowing he was there beside her. Then when she awakened and found it wasn't the same wishful dream, a great joy filled her. Josh was there next to her, his vital warmth burning its way through her nightgown. She couldn't keep pretending that she didn't want him any more. She had to feel his intimate touch! And once he caressed her, Sabrina knew she had to have his full possession. Nothing else mattered. All the feeble resolutions she had tried to make were swept away by the hot tide of passion that engulfed her.

Raising herself higher in bed, she leaned over him, framing his face in her palms. Her hair fell in a golden mantle around his bare shoulders as she lowered her head to cover his mouth with her avid one.

Sabrina's eyes gleamed between thick lashes. "Do you still think I'm sleeping, Josh?" she whispered softly.

His intake of breath was almost painful. Linking his hand around the back of her neck, he stared up at her in the darkened room. "Are you sure, Sabrina?"

The tip of her tongue delicately outlined the shape of his firm mouth before probing at his closed lips. "Don't you want to make love to me, Josh?"

His rigid control was in danger of slipping. It was evident in the hoarseness of his voice. "You know the answer to that. I just don't want you to have any regrets tomorrow."

"It's already tomorrow." Sabrina smiled, sliding the ribbon straps of her nightgown down her arms, exposing pearly skin that gleamed in the moonlight.

Josh reached for her, crushing her against him in a fierce

42

embrace. "My love." He groaned. "You'll never know how often I've dreamed about this!"

His hand tangled in her hair, holding her for a deep, sensual kiss that expressed his great longing. Sabrina returned it ardently, straining to get closer to him.

His mouth trailed a shivery path down to her waist where the nightgown was bunched. Slipping an arm under her, he lifted Sabrina's body, sliding the filmy gown over her hips and down her long legs. His hands made it a seduction, lingering tantalizingly each step of the way, promising but not fulfilling.

She arched her body in an attempt at closer contact, and Josh obliged eagerly. His hands sent waves of excitement raging through her, stoking the fire that threatened to burn out of control. Sabrina pulled him on top of her, needing to feel the hard male contours she remembered so intimately.

"My sweet, passionate Sabrina," Josh breathed, sliding his hands beneath her. Cupping her bottom, he pressed her hips tightly against his throbbing loins.

She moved against him in an agony of desire. "Love me, Josh. Love me now!"

With a cry of exultation deep in his throat, he hastened to comply. Parting her legs, Josh wrapped his arms around her as their bodies joined in the first exquisite union. Sabrina was immediately filled with such rapture that her slender body was racked with it. She rose again and again to meet the driving male force that reached for the core of her being, carrying her to frenzied heights.

Each dizzying spiral was more intense than the last, until finally they reached the summit of sensation together. After a burst of almost unbearable delight, they began the long descent clasped in each other's arms, both totally fulfilled.

Josh's heart gradually slowed, the steady beat entering

Sabrina's breast and merging with her own. His lips clung to hers. They were joined in every way possible.

After a long time she stirred, rubbing her cheek against the thick mat of dark hair that cushioned his hard chest. "I think I'd forgotten it could be that wonderful." She sighed softly.

Josh kissed the tip of her nose, caressing her gently. "Give me a few minutes and I'll refresh your memory." He chuckled.

Sabrina pulled his hair playfully. "Don't think I won't remind you."

It was a night to remember the rest of her life. They made love over and over again, with a hunger born of months apart. When at last they fell asleep, it was joined together, as though neither could bear to be separated from the other.

The sun was high in the sky when Sabrina finally awoke. As consciousness slowly returned and she became aware of Josh's firm shoulder beneath her cheek, her heart filled with joy. It hadn't been one of those dreams that left her aching. The languorously satisfied state of her body attested to that.

Tilting her head to look at Josh's patrician features, relaxed now in sleep, Sabrina resisted the urge to kiss him awake. The poor man needed his rest, she reflected in stifled amusement. How many times had he brought her to fulfillment last night? She frowned in concentration.

Josh's eyes flew open, as if aware of her scrutiny. His eager smile died as he looked at her frowning face.

"Good morning," she murmured, suddenly shy that she had been caught staring at him.

"Is it, Sabrina?" Josh asked carefully, watching her intently, his face almost stern.

"I . . . what do you mean?"

"You aren't regretting last night, are you?"

44

"How can you even ask such a question?"

Relief chased away all other emotion as he gathered her close. "You were frowning . . . I thought . . ."

"Silly!" Sabrina's deep, ardent kiss was more reassuring than any words. Suddenly she started to giggle.

"What's so funny?" he demanded.

"You are." Her green eyes were bright with mischief. "You asked why I was frowning."

He arched an imperious eyebrow. "Are you going to tell me or let me worry all day?"

"I was trying to remember how many times you made love to me," she admitted, her fingers moving over his stomach in a feathery caress.

Josh's reaction was instantaneous. His tawny eyes glowed with wicked intention. "Whatever number you came up with—add one more," he ordered, pulling her body firmly to his.

Sabrina moved out of his arms. "You promised to take me to Keukenhoff Gardens today."

"Later," he growled, reaching for her again.

It was a temptation, but she resisted. After all, they would have two glorious weeks alone. "It's almost noon already."

He caught her around the waist as she was preparing to slide out of bed. "I want to make love to you in the daylight so I can see every delicious inch of you."

When he tossed aside the covers, his burning gaze sweeping over her body, Sabrina felt the same old magic starting to work. And when his warm mouth traveled a shivery path down her length, pausing for enflaming kisses, her resistance was gone.

"You win, Josh." She sighed. "Something tells me I'm not going to get out of this hotel room today."

His mouth stopped tormenting her. Josh lifted his head, ruffling her hair fondly. "I'm sorry, sweetheart. I just can't

45

get enough of you. But you're right—a promise is a promise. I'll turn on the shower for us."

He was gone before Sabrina could tell him she had changed her mind. She turned on her side, hugging his pillow. It was almost scary to be this happy!

"Come on in, the water's just right," Josh called from the bathroom.

Sabrina joined him in the shower, taking Josh's outstretched hand as she stepped over the edge of the large, old-fashioned bathtub. When he pulled the shower curtain around, they were enclosed in a private, steamy world.

Sabrina fully expected to make it speedy, but when Josh insisted on washing her, she knew what the outcome would be. His hands were unbearably sensuous as he soaped her all over, lifting her leg to reach the soft white skin of her inner thigh. She couldn't help seeing how it affected him, and her own body reacted in kind.

"I'm sorry, darling." Josh groaned. "Maybe you'd better get out of here and get some clothes on."

She ran her hands down his splendid, supple frame, touching him as she knew he longed to be touched. A shudder rippled through him, along with a wordless cry of satisfaction. Josh reached for a pile of towels on a rack, dropping them into the tub and guiding Sabrina down onto them. He covered her body with his, moving against her with pulsating desire.

The soft towels cushioned her back and the warm spray caressed her as Josh once more staked his masculine claim, carrying her into a fiery world that no water could quench. The climax of their passion was so intense that they were shaken by it, lying in the gentle rain until they could catch their breath.

Later, Sabrina thought anything would be a letdown after such a night and morning, but Keukenhoff Gardens proved to be the delight she had been looking forward to.

On the way, they passed acre upon acre of tulips, flowing in a straight line like an improbable, technicolor river. Vivid slashes of red were banded by pink and purple and yellow.

"It's incredible!" Sabrina gasped.

"Wait till you get to the gardens," Josh advised. "As the man said, 'You ain't seen nothin' yet.' "

The massive park was filled with glowing beds of hyacinths and daffodils, their soft blue and gold complementing the brighter tulips. Benches were thoughtfully placed along the paths that cut through the well-tended lawns, shaded by feathery dogwood trees in full pink and white bloom. When Sabrina had walked until her legs ached, they sat down on a bench facing a pond where regal swans lifted their heads like disdainful royalty.

Sabrina shook her head in wonder. "It has to be seen to be believed."

"Now aren't you glad I made you get out of bed?" Josh asked mischievously.

"How can you say a thing like that with a straight face?" she demanded indignantly. "We'd still be in our birthday suits if it weren't for me!"

Josh lifted her hand, kissing the palm. "Any complaints?"

"Not a one," she murmured softly as their eyes held.

"You'll have to be strong for both of us," he told her with a smile. "There are a lot of other things I want to show you."

She sighed happily. "This was my first choice. You know how I love flowers."

"Would you like to buy some tulip bulbs to take home? The gardener can plant them outside our bedroom window so you can see them first thing in the morning."

Sabrina stared at him with parted lips. She hadn't even thought about the future. For the first time she realized how different it was going to be. Was it possible that they could actually live together again? Did Josh really want her or was he still just using her?

"How about it?" Josh eyed her questioningly.

"Oh, the tulips . . ." She gathered herself together nervously. Josh must never know how much he meant to her. If he realized it was love she felt, and not the desire that was obvious, his hold over her would be complete. "Will . . . uh . . . will they grow in California?"

"Sure. They ship them with complete instructions in the fall. You and the gardener can spend long, happy hours babying them," he told her fondly.

Sabrina hesitated. "I don't expect to have long hours to spend in the yard," she said finally.

"What do you mean?" He frowned slightly.

"I intend to continue working."

"In New York?" he asked incredulously.

"No, of course not. I'll get a job in Los Angeles."

"What for?" he demanded.

"Because I need to," she answered quietly.

"That's the most ridiculous thing I ever heard! Have I ever denied you anything?"

"No, you've been more than generous." Sabrina thought of the furs and jewelry Josh had lavished on her.

"Then what's all this nonsense about needing money?"

"I didn't say that." She concentrated on smoothing the skirt over her knee, a small stab of apprehension piercing her. Sabrina was reluctant to let anything intrude on their new-found bliss. Why did it have to come up today?

Josh raised her chin, turning her face to his. "If it isn't money, then what is it?"

"Try to understand, Josh. For the first time in my life I know what it is to be independent, and I like the feeling."

A muscle worked at the point of his square jaw. "Independent of me," he stated flatly.

"No! Not only you. Can't you see? Simon brought me up like a little princess. I never learned anything more useful than French. He made all my decisions for me, and then when I was nineteen I married you—another strong man."

"Are you saying I dominated you?" Josh was honestly trying to understand. "If I was dictatorial, believe me, Sabrina, it wasn't intentional. You had only to call me on it."

"You were wonderful to me." She bent her head, remembering. "I was happy until . . ."

"Sabrina, about Pam that night—" Josh began urgently.

"I don't want to talk about it," she interrupted firmly.

The misery of the night Josh had lied about being with the other woman was still with Sabrina, but she had resolved to close her mind to it. The worst part of his infidelity was that it made his real reasons for desiring her all too apparent. It wasn't her he wanted, it was her name. But the one thing she had discovered last night was that she couldn't give Josh up again. Talking about it would only open old wounds and threaten her new happiness. She couldn't know the anguish that decision would cost her.

"I want to explain why I'm going to get a job," she said carefully. "When I left you that night I went back to Grandfather's house, expecting to be welcomed with open arms. Instead, he was furious that I intended to get a divorce. He asked me what I expected to live on, because he said he wouldn't take me back."

"I don't believe it." Josh scowled.

"I realize now that he was only bluffing. He wanted me to return to you, and that seemed like a sure-fire way. But at the time, I was hurt and angry. I packed a bag, taking only the barest necessities, and I bought a ticket to New York."

"Where did you get the money? You didn't withdraw anything from our checking account."

"I didn't want to take anything from either of you," she answered simply. When he waited, she added reluctantly. "I sold my mother's jewelry. It was the only thing that belonged to me."

Josh's grip on her folded hands was almost paralyzing. "If you're trying to make me feel like a monster, you've succeeded. Why didn't you accept alimony, Sabrina? I tried to get my lawyer to force it on you. When you wouldn't touch it, I thought at least Simon was taking care of you."

"I wouldn't have let him either. After taking a long look at myself, I found that I didn't like what I saw. Nobody should be as useless as I was. It was a terrible shock, but at least it forced me into remedying the situation. My finances didn't allow me the luxury of going to school to learn a skill, so I took stock of my assets and did the next best thing." She gave him a little smile. "You know that old adage: If all you've got are lemons, make lemonade."

Josh's answering smile was full of love. "I've always thought of you more as a peach." His voice dropped to a husky note. "A ripe, fragrant, beautiful peach."

She leaned her forehead against his, inhaling the wonderful male aroma of him. "Is that a romantic way of saying I'm a tasty dish?" she teased.

He winked at her seductively. "I'll show you just how tasty when we get back to the hotel."

Sabrina's heart suddenly skipped a beat. Josh could awaken her with just a few words. It was a little frightening to be this much in love with a man.

"In the meantime, finish your story," he said.

"You know the rest. I got a job and learned the value of money." She gazed reflectively at a yellow tulip striped

50

with scarlet. "I can hardly believe that my coming-out dress cost the equivalent of a month's rent."

Josh shrugged. "Everything is relative. To Simon it was about the same as buying a good cigar."

"I suppose so, but after earning my own way, I don't think I could ever be that extravagant again."

"You never were," he told her fondly. "I was the one who wanted you to have expensive things."

The diamond necklace flashed into both their minds. "I'm sorry," Sabrina murmured, lowering her lashes. "I wasn't very gracious last night."

"I wasn't exactly Sir Galahad myself." His hand slid under her bright hair, his long fingers massaging her neck muscles sensuously. "But I'd say we both made up for it."

Sabrina gave herself up to the pleasure of his touch, uttering a small sound of contentment. "I do love the necklace, Josh. I'll wear it everywhere—even to work."

His fingers stopped their labor of love. "You mean you seriously think you need to get a job?"

"I just explained it to you. I thought you understood."

"I do understand. You wanted to prove that you could stand on your own two feet, and you did it. I realize it's a tremendous satisfaction, and I'm proud of you. But now that we're back together again, what's the point?"

"The point is that I want to be a person in my own right, not just an adjunct to you! You have your life—I want to have mine."

"I've always shared mine with you," he said steadily.

They were skating perilously close to the edge. Sabrina veered away from reminding him, her eyes falling before his compelling gaze. "I have to have something meaningful to do with my days. I can't go back to the same old aimless life of shopping and lunch."

"What do you plan to do?"

51

"I thought maybe I could get a job with an export company or perhaps be a translator for a publishing firm."

"Have you thought of doing volunteer work with one of the agencies that deals with exchange students?" Josh asked quietly.

"No, I—I want to be—" She stopped before using the word "independent" again. It obviously had a negative connotation to Josh. And possibly he was right.

Much as she railed against it, the thought was in the back of Sabrina's mind. If things didn't work out between them, she would have something to fall back on. Because she was through running away. There wasn't any place far enough to obliterate the memory of Josh. Impatiently, Sabrina threw off the depression that caused. Nothing was going to go wrong. She just had to convince Josh that their marriage would be better if she had something rewarding to do, as he did.

"I want to be paid for my services," she explained earnestly. "Maybe it's because I've never worked until now, but you'll never know how I felt when I got my first paycheck. I felt like an amateur athlete turning pro."

Josh folded her in his arms, oblivious to the people passing by. "I think I do know how you felt, and I'm bursting with pride. My only regret is that I wasn't there to share the moment with you."

She rested her head on his reassuring shoulder. "Then you don't mind?"

"I'll have to admit I'd rather have you home waiting for me, all rested and eager instead of frazzled around the edges from having to put up with some guy like me all day. But since that makes me the ultimate male chauvinist, I'll agree to share you—to a limited extent," he added, looking down at her sternly.

She fluttered her lashes at him. "Whatever do you mean?"

"Don't give me that wide-eyed innocent act." Josh kissed her hard. "You're mine, and don't you ever forget it."

If only he were as completely hers! Their sexual attraction was breathtaking, but Sabrina wanted more—she wanted his love.

Josh tipped her chin up with a long forefinger, searching her face with narrowed eyes. "Hey, don't look so sad. Is the idea that distasteful?"

She mustered a smile. "About as horrendous as a triple banana split."

Josh knew that was her favorite. His tense expression relaxed. "With hot fudge sauce, whipped cream, and a cherry?"

She closed her eyes in ecstasy. "What could be better?"

"Perhaps I can think of something," he murmured huskily in her ear, as they rose to make their way back out of the gardens.

There was a stack of phone messages when they returned to the hotel. Josh tore them up one after the other, his secret smile at Sabrina starting a flutter in the pit of her stomach.

"Can you imagine people bothering us on our honeymoon?" His low voice was like a caress. "Maybe I'll get back to them in five or six days—just maybe."

The last slip of paper wiped the smile from his face. It was a message to call the hospital in Los Angeles.

"Oh, Josh, do you think Grandfather's had another attack?" Sabrina whispered, her face stricken.

"There's no reason to assume that, honey." Josh was outwardly reassuring, but he couldn't quite hide his own apprehension. "We'll go up to the room and put in a call."

While they were waiting for the trans-Atlantic operator to place the call, Josh tried to conceal his concern from Sabrina. It was evident though, in the tautness of his long body and the number of cigarettes he smoked. When the phone rang, he reached it on the first ring.

"I'm sorry, but Mr. Sheffield can't talk to anyone right now." Even the nurse's voice was starchy. "He's having his temperature taken."

"Give me the damn phone!" Simon's roar was audible in the background.

"Will you *please* put that thermometer back in your mouth!" The nurse's patience sounded as if it were near the breaking point.

"How long do you people have to test before you know if I'm done enough?" Simon's patience was in an even more precarious state. "If you don't stop pestering me, I'm going to buy this poor excuse for a hospital and turn it into a home for retired go-go dancers! Hello!" he shouted into the phone.

Josh started to laugh. Turning to Sabrina, he said, "I don't think you have to worry about Simon having an attack—the nurses maybe, but not your grandfather."

"Who is this?" Simon demanded. "Speak up, I don't have all day!"

"I wasn't aware that you were going anywhere." Josh chuckled. "How are you, chief? Although I believe I already know."

"Josh? It's good to hear your voice, son." The older man greeted him with genuine warmth.

"Yours too. How's it going?"

"Terrible! The figures on the Caldecott Company are down, and I'm not sure Tom is working out. Maybe we shouldn't have brought him along so fast."

"I didn't mean that," Josh commented mildly. "I was referring to your health."

"There's nothing wrong with me any more," Simon answered fretfully. "If those doctors weren't so reluctant to let go of a good thing, I'd be out of this asylum. They're keeping me a prisoner here." At an audible gasp in the background, he addressed the unseen nurse. "Well, it's true. Isn't that why you took away my clothes and gave me this indecent gown to wear? How can I escape knowing my fanny is on prominent display?"

Josh tried unsuccessfully to stifle his laughter. "Couldn't you go a little easier on the nurses, Simon?"

"What are you talking about? They love me!" He chuckled unexpectedly. "The ones who take care of me get combat pay."

Josh knew that Simon was aware of the selfless dedication of the staff when he needed them. He also knew the older man would find a way of rewarding them all handsomely.

Sabrina couldn't restrain herself any longer. "Let me talk to him," she begged. When Josh handed her the receiver she asked anxiously, "Are you sure you're all right, Grandfather?"

"Tiptop, sweetheart," he told her fondly.

"We were so worried when there was a message to call the hospital."

"Oh, that. I got lonesome." Simon shrugged off the trans-Atlantic call as if it were something everyone did to pass the time. "It's hell to be old and all alone," he added plaintively.

Sabrina knew it was a blatant bid for sympathy. Simon was not only conducting business from his command post in the hospital, he probably also had hordes of visitors. Her conscience bothered her, however. "Would you like us to come home?" she asked uncertainly.

"Where did you get an idea like that? This is your honeymoon." After a barely perceptible pause, he inquired casually, "How is everything working out?"

Sabrina looked across the room at Josh, who was removing his jacket. The familiar sight of his broad shoulders tapering to narrow hips and a flat stomach was something she would never get enough of. She tried to match Simon's offhand tone. "We're holding up fairly well."

That didn't satisfy him in the least. "What's that supposed to mean? Is something wrong? You're not arguing again, are you?" Simon asked sharply.

"No, nothing like that," she assured him hastily. Sabrina's sweet mouth curved in a smile of pure happiness. It didn't make any difference if Simon knew the truth. "Everything's just wonderful," she said softly. "I'm very happy, Grandfather."

His relief was evidenced by the bluster in his voice. "Well, I'm glad you finally came to your senses. Didn't I tell you Josh was a good man?"

Sabrina bubbled with laughter. "Even you don't know *how* good!"

"What kind of talk is that for a well brought up young lady?" Simon pretended to be shocked, but he couldn't sustain the pose. "What the hell, you're on your honeymoon." He chuckled. "Let me speak to Josh again."

After Sabrina called Josh from the bedroom, she went in to take off her own things.

"If you're going to discuss business, forget it, Simon." Josh smiled. "I promised Sabrina I wouldn't even think about Ameropol for the next two weeks."

"That isn't why I called." Simon was deadly serious, all role playing and temperament gone. "How is it working out between you two?"

"Couldn't be better. You were right—as usual."

"She sounded happy," Simon said tentatively.

Josh's warm smile held remembrance. "I think you can safely say that."

The older man seemed to need reassurance. "That child is my whole life, Josh. Her happiness is paramount with me. I would never have done anything I didn't honestly believe was in her best interest."

"I know."

"If I didn't think you were the right man for her, it would be different." There was almost a question in the statement.

"Don't worry about a thing, Simon. We're back together for good. I intend to be very careful this time." Josh gave a rueful laugh. "She isn't as trusting as she used to be. If she ever found out—" He glanced up to see Sabrina standing in the doorway. Without any change of expression, Josh continued smoothly. "There isn't anything to be concerned about. I'll cover all bases." There was an underlying urgency in his voice as he added, "Just stay out of it from now on, Simon."

Sabrina stood very still, clutching two dresses over her arm. She had intended to ask Josh's opinion on which to wear that evening. The tail end of his conversation drove everything else out of her mind. Who were they talking about? If they were referring to her, what was it she mustn't find out?

Josh hung up the phone, turning to her with an easy smile. "There, I told you that you were worried for nothing. Simon sounded like his old, hell-raising self."

"What were you two discussing there at the end?" With a great effort, Sabrina kept her voice even.

Josh shrugged. "You can never keep Simon off business completely. He's concerned about some woman who holds a large block of preferred stock. She's being difficult, but I told him I'd handle it."

Sabrina wanted desperately to believe him. As she stared up into his dark, handsome face, she was torn in two directions. Josh had lied to her before. He had taken Pam to dinner when he was supposedly working. Was the affair still going on? Since Pam was a department head at Ameropol, it wouldn't be too difficult to engineer. Was that what Sabrina mustn't be allowed to find out?

But surely her own grandfather wouldn't countenance such a thing! Sabrina felt a cold chill as she realized he just might—if he saw it as an unimportant, purely sexual outlet. They were both highly successful men of the world. Sabrina had heard stories about Simon's own reputation with women. Her grandfather's first concern was with her own happiness and second with the business. Josh was his trusted lieutenant. If he made Sabrina happy, Simon wouldn't be too judgmental about things he considered purely recreational.

And as long as Josh knew he wasn't jeopardizing his goal of taking over Ameropol, he didn't see any reason to change his philandering ways—as long as he was careful. *She isn't as trusting as she used to be.* The words hammered at Sabrina's brain.

Josh stroked her long, fair hair lovingly. When she flinched away from him, his eyes narrowed. "What is it, Sabrina?"

She drew a shuddering breath before posing the question she had vowed never to ask. "Are you still having an affair with Pam Welby?"

When he hesitated, Sabrina felt as if she were suffocating. Then Josh said, "I suppose it's pointless to say I never had an affair with Pam, so I'll answer your question. No, I'm not having an affair with Pam Welby."

He put his arms around her rigid shoulders, drawing her against him. Sabrina held herself stiffly, refusing to allow his blatant masculinity to seduce her. He raised her chin, feathering light kisses across her closed eyelids, down the curve of her cheek to her mouth, where he nibbled gently on her lower lip.

"Didn't last night and this morning tell you anything, my beautiful bride?" His hands trailed down her back to

58

press her hips close to his, so that she was achingly aware of him.

Sabrina swallowed hard. "I know you want me, Josh, but—"

"All the time." He groaned, moving against her in exquisite suggestion.

Tiny flames of fire licked at her body. Before they could rage out of control, she cried, "If you were talking about me, you were right. I'm *not* as trusting as I used to be! And I won't share you."

Josh chuckled deep in his throat. "I don't expect to have any energy left over for that sort of thing."

He swept her into his arms, ignoring her protests as he strode masterfully toward the bedroom. When he joined her on the bed, stroking her body with tantalizing caresses, Sabrina throbbed with an urgent desire she couldn't suppress. Josh's murmured words in her ear completed the seduction. She surrendered with a sigh.

Much later, Sabrina looked down at Josh's beloved head on her breast. She had to believe him. This man was as essential to her as the air she breathed. And she must mean something to him too. She had to be more than just his path to power.

With a silent prayer, Sabrina drifted off to sleep.

CHAPTER FOUR

Sabrina was reluctant to see their idyllic honeymoon end and had to wonder how the two weeks had gone by so quickly, but it was a joy to return to the beautiful home she had presided over so briefly.

When the taxi pulled up in front of the luxurious, sprawling redwood house, Josh murmured, "Welcome home, Mrs. Winchester."

Although it was late, there were lights streaming through the wide windows, casting a glow that was reflected in Sabrina's heart. The front door was opened by a smiling Japanese couple. Akira and Michiko had been with Josh for years. The fact that they had waited up for them expressed their happiness at her return. There were tears in Sabrina's eyes as Josh swung her into his arms and carried her over the threshold.

"Michiko and I wish to welcome you back, Mrs. Winchester." Akira echoed Josh's sentiment.

"Thank you, Akira, it's good to be here," she answered softly.

Everything was exactly as she remembered it. Except for the pile of luggage by the front door, they might have been returning from an evening on the town. When Josh put his arm around her shoulders and led her down the hall to the master bedroom, the feeling was heightened.

The covers on the king-size bed had been turned down

as they always were when they came home. The crystal lamps on either side of the bed cast a soft light on the pale-blue silk sheets and down comforter. There were two yellow roses in the slender bud vase she had always kept filled on her dressing table—and there was something else. The half-empty bottles of perfume she hadn't taken were exactly where she had left them.

Josh answered her startled look in a voice husky with emotion. "I told Michiko to leave them there because they reminded me of you."

"Would you have forgotten me if she'd have moved them?" Sabrina knew the answer, she just wanted to hear him say it.

He reached for her, burying his face in the curve of her neck. "How can you forget an ache that tears at your insides night and day? I used to lie in bed and imagine you were there beside me." His hands wandered down her body, tracing every curve lingeringly. "I'd close my eyes and pretend I was touching you. I remembered how soft your skin was and the little things that gave you pleasure."

Sabrina's blood raced to meet his caressing hands. She wound her arms around his neck, whispering in his ear, "They still do, and you don't have to pretend any more."

He lifted her effortlessly, carrying her over to the bed. Just before he put her down his arms tightened and he stared at her. The expression on his face was almost stern. "I won't ever let you go again, Sabrina."

The next morning, the sound of the alarm clock was an unaccustomed intrusion. For the past two weeks their mornings had been slow awakenings filled with leisurely delight.

Josh reached over quickly to silence the alarm before it woke Sabrina, but her eyelids fluttered. She snuggled closer to him. "What time is it?"

61

He kissed the tip of her nose. "It's early, darling, go back to sleep."

As he stuck one long leg out from beneath the covers, she opened her eyes fully. "Where are you going?"

"To work."

Sabrina sat up, now fully awake. "But it's our first day back."

"And Simon will have a dozen projects waiting for me. I'm going to stop by his house before I go to the office."

"He shouldn't even be home from the hospital, much less conducting business," she remarked disapprovingly.

"Are you kidding? The doctors would have had to approach him with a whip and a chair if they hadn't given in."

Sabrina smiled at the truth in that as Josh walked across the room, unashamedly nude. "I suppose this means the honeymoon's over." She sighed.

He came back to sit on the edge of the bed, hooking his hand around the back of her neck. "Don't you believe it. It's never going to be over." His mouth met hers, parting her lips in a slow seduction.

Sabrina's body responded to him as it always did. But when she put her arms around his neck, tantalizing his bare chest with the tips of her breasts, Josh untangled her arms reluctantly.

"Don't tempt me, love. I'm going to need all my strength today."

Josh was right, of course. They couldn't spend the rest of their lives in bed. In a way she was glad he knew that too, and she silently hoped that for him, there *was* more to their relationship than sex.

Simon looked wonderful when she visited him later in the day, declaring his intention to return to the office soon —which Sabrina didn't doubt for a moment. He was capable of breaking all the rules and getting away with it. She was reassured by the robustness of his health, and Simon was delighted by the obvious happiness shining out of her face. It was a good visit.

By the next morning Sabrina felt as if she had never been away. The suitcases were unpacked, everything put in its place, and she and Josh were having breakfast together as they used to. He was swallowing a last bit of coffee, wearing the intent, eager look he always wore when he was going to work.

As she watched him leave Sabrina suddenly realized that she had no plans for the day. What on earth had she done with her time before? When the phone rang a short time later, she remembered.

"I heard you were back." It was Melanie Livingston, an old friend. "We were so excited when we found out about you and Josh. You're a fine friend! Why didn't you tell me?"

"Well, it . . . it all happened so fast."

"That's no excuse, but I'll forgive you if you have lunch with me today and tell me all the delicious details. How about meeting at the club at one? I have a tennis lesson at twelve so I'll be in my grubbies, but you won't mind, will you?"

"No, of course not," Sabrina answered automatically.

"We have the most divine new tennis pro. He's absolutely to die over! You'll have to join our Tuesday morning foursome," Melanie continued without stopping for a breath. "You can have your old place back because Cookie is dropping out. She's pregnant again, can you believe it?"

"Really?" Sabrina murmured, when some response seemed called for.

Melanie laughed. "We all think she did it to get out of serving on another one of Shelley's committees. Hold out for the Opera Guild when Shelley nails you. That's the only one that's any fun."

"I'm not sure—" Sabrina began.

"Oh, another thing before I forget," Melanie interrupted. "For heaven's sake, don't invite Dede and Kim to the same party. They had the most awful row at the country club dance. I'll fill you in on the whole thing over lunch. You just can't imagine all that's happened since you've been gone."

"About lunch, Melanie—I just remembered that I have a . . . an appointment at the dentist. I won't be able to make it today."

After she finally managed to get off the phone, Sabrina was appalled. Had she actually spent her days like Melanie? Working in New York had been so absorbing that she had almost forgotten her former idle existence.

Sabrina had intended to take a week to get things in order before looking for a job, but she suddenly realized that everything had already been taken care of. With a gleam of purpose in her eyes, she opened the morning newspaper to the help-wanted ads.

Since she didn't know exactly what she was searching for, Sabrina looked first under translator, then under both tutor and interpreter. None of them yielded any prospects. When she couldn't think of any other category, her soft mouth set grimly. If she had to start at the top and read every ad in the paper, so be it. Somewhere in Los Angeles there was a job she could fill.

Sabrina struck paydirt in the *A's*. An advertisement for an associate editor carried the requirement: "Must be fluent in French." The fact that she had no idea of an associate editor's function didn't bother her a bit. She filled half of the qualifications!

The office she headed for a short time later was in a tall building on Wilshire Boulevard, not far from Ameropol's corporate headquarters. Sabrina's adrenaline was pumping at a furious rate as she walked past the futuristic sculpture rising above a splashing fountain in the courtyard. If determination counted for anything, she was going to get the job.

In spite of her confidence, Sabrina was in a state of joyous shock when she retraced her steps after the interview. It had gone very well, and somehow she just knew she would be hired for what promised to be the most fascinating job imaginable! Her first impulse was to race over to Josh's office to share her excitement, but she restrained herself. Sabrina knew what his working day was like—several telephones ringing at once and a dozen people asking his advice. This merited his full attention.

By the time Josh got home that night, Sabrina was in a fever of impatience. As soon as she had returned home the call had come—she had the job! To celebrate, she had changed into a long flowing caftan of gauzy sari cloth shot through with gold threads that glinted like the soft blond hair curling around her shoulders. Excitement turned her eyes an even deeper green, and her mouth kept curving in a bewitching smile.

The tired lines vanished from Josh's face when he came into the den and Sabrina threw herself in his arms. They tightened around her as he buried his face in the fragrant golden cloud of her hair.

"Now this is what I call the perfect ending to a day," he murmured.

"Oh, Josh, I thought you'd *never* come home!"

His hands moved down her back, searching out the slim body under the filmy material. "That's the kind of reception I like to hear." He began to draw her nearer, to imprison her in his embrace.

For once Sabrina was immune. "Later, Josh. I want to talk to you."

"Is anything wrong, Sabrina?" Josh's smile vanished as he searched her flushed face.

"No, everything is perfect. I got a job today!" She had intended to lead up to it but the wonderful news burst out.

Josh's reaction was less than enthralled. "What was the big hurry?" He frowned. "We just got home a couple of days ago. You need some time to rest up.".

"Why should I need a rest after a vacation? You certainly didn't. Besides, I'm not some little hothouse flower." Sabrina's impatience fled as she returned to the subject. "Wait until you hear about it. I'm going to be an associate editor, no less! This new magazine is starting up—well, actually it isn't new. *La Vie* has been publishing in France and England, and they've just decided to expand to the United States. They'll be buying some material here, but the main thrust will be stories and articles about the Continent. I'll be translating them. Isn't that fantastic?"

Josh moved to the bar, where he poured himself a drink. "If that's what you want."

She stared at his back indignantly. "This is the greatest thing that ever happened to me and you're acting as though I just offered you a black kitty with a white stripe down its back!"

"Perhaps I want to be the greatest thing that ever happened to you," he returned evenly.

"You *are* emotionally, Josh! But one thing has nothing to do with the other."

"Doesn't it, Sabrina? Aren't you taking out insurance in case you want to leave me again?"

As she looked at the deep lines carved in his rugged face, Sabrina felt her anger fading. Had Josh suffered as much as she during their separation? She took the drink out of his hand and put it on the bar. Sliding her fingers through his thick, dark hair, she ruffled it lovingly.

"Why would I do a thing like that now that I have you nicely broken in? Besides, I've already explained to you my need for a job." She looked into his eyes, imploring him to understand.

He gathered her so tightly in his arms that she had trouble breathing. "I'm sorry, darling. I know I'm a selfish lout but I can't help it. I don't want to share you with anyone."

"I share *you*, Josh. You have a whole full life outside of this house but it doesn't take anything away from me. When you come home at night you're all mine. And that's the way it will be with me too."

The eagerness in her face convinced him of its importance to her. Josh tried to mask his unhappiness with a forced smile. "Promise you won't start working late at the office with one of those hand-kissing Frenchmen?"

Sabrina slowly untied his tie, looking up at him through long lashes. "Not if you make it worth my while to come home."

Her new job proved to be a turning point in Sabrina's life. She was filled with purpose, greeting each new day with anticipation. There was so much to learn. The magazine introduced her to the world of business as well as the arts, and she soaked up the complicated details like a sponge. Josh had never discussed business with her and she began to wonder why.

"Because when I'm with you I'm not interested in facts, only figures," he teased, when she asked him the question.

"If that's supposed to be flattering, it isn't! I happen to have a brain, in addition to my other moving parts."

They were sitting on the couch in the den after dinner. Josh put his arm around her shoulder, pulling her closer. "And I'm sure it's as delectable as the rest of you."

Sabrina pulled away, looking at him coolly. "It appears that's going to remain my little secret."

When he realized she was serious, Josh's smile faded. "What's bothering you, honey?"

"You are! Can't you see I want to be treated like a woman, not the favorite teddy bear you take to bed every night? Most husbands talk to their wives. They bring their problems home and discuss them. But you keep your business world separate—as though you think I'm not intelligent enough to understand."

"You know that's not true, darling!"

"No, I don't," she answered slowly. "I know you're not a typical male chauvinist. You've placed women in positions of authority. I've seen the interest on your face when you talk to them. That's what I want to share with you, don't you see?"

"I don't really have any problems," he answered helplessly.

"That's not true, every business has problems. Besides, I know something's been worrying you lately. Well, maybe not worrying you, but you've been rather abstract at times."

He gave her a startled look. "I wasn't aware that it showed. It isn't anything serious, just a little difficulty with the Cranmar Company. It's a pharmaceutical company as you know, and someone's filed a big lawsuit. We're completely blameless but the adverse publicity has affected sales."

Sabrina resolutely kept the discussion on business, determined to prove her mental worth to Josh. "Surely a conglomerate as big as Ameropol isn't affected severely by a temporary loss in one area?"

"No, but every company is supposed to pull its own weight."

"If the product is really blameless, why don't you issue a guarantee?"

"We already do, but nobody seems to be reading the fine print on the bottle."

"Then why don't you publicize it? Take out big ads and

assure the public that the company stands behind its product."

He shook his head. "Publicity about pharmaceutical companies can cause the stock to plunge. We've been keeping a low profile, waiting for things to return to normal."

"And how far has that gotten you? If I'd been a satisfied customer before, I'd have an open mind. All it would take to get my business back would be reassurance."

"You might be right at that; maybe we should have been fighting back," Josh said slowly. He got up to pace the floor with rising enthusiasm. "It's only a nuisance suit. The stock will recover once people start buying again."

"And you can always justify a bad quarter with a tax loss," she agreed encouragingly.

Josh stopped pacing to look at her incredulously. "Where did you ever learn about things like tax credits?"

"I don't spend all my time at work having my hand kissed," she remarked dryly.

"You'd better not spend any of it that way." He framed her face in his palms. "That's my exclusive privilege in this marriage."

"And what's mine, Josh?" Sabrina asked, looking up at him steadily. "What's my role?"

"Yours is to educate a poor dumb male who always realized he had the smartest woman in the world but was too stupid to tell her so."

"I don't want you to tell me." She had to be sure he understood. "I want you to show me."

"From now on, sweetheart, you're going to be my consultant. I'll even give you a job if you want it."

"I already have one. Two," she corrected herself, kissing the hollow in his throat. "The other is educating a big, dumb male who doesn't know when the victor is ready for her rewards."

Josh scooped her up in his arms, looking into her lovely

69

face with deep emotion. "I'm the one who is getting the reward—every day since you came back to me."

After that night Sabrina went from happy to blissful. Josh was as good as his word. He discussed things with her, listening intently to her opinions. Sometimes she contributed valuable advice, while other times Josh pointed out why her suggestions weren't feasible. But Sabrina had the satisfaction of knowing he was taking her seriously.

They had breakfast together every morning, going over their plans for the day and evening. But one morning Sabrina was already dressed and ready to leave by the time Josh got out of the shower.

"Why are you rushing off this early?" he complained.

"I have to meet Jacques Tresante at the airport," she explained. "He's a very prestigious author in France. We're serializing his new novel. It's a real coup for the magazine."

"Why doesn't he take a taxi?" Josh growled.

"You, of all people, know about V.I.P. treatment," Sabrina chided him. "Monsieur Tresante expects the best."

"He's certainly getting it." Josh pulled her close, nuzzling the soft hair away from her ear so he could explore the inner contours with his tongue. "How about letting Monsieur Tresante find his own way to the office? If he's smart enough to write a best seller, he can surely hail a cab."

It was a temptation that Sabrina had to resist. "Do you want to destroy Franco-American relations?" she teased. "Not to mention my job. If I don't keep Monsieur Tresante happy, my head will be on prominent display in the reception area."

"Just how happy do you plan on keeping him?" Josh asked with a raised eyebrow.

"Something along the lines of last night," she replied impishly.

"That settles it, you're not leaving this house," Josh declared, dumping her on the bed.

"Josh, I have to go," Sabrina protested, laughing. "I'll see you tonight, but I might be late. Just don't let your imagination run away with you."

"You'll be back in time for the premiere?"

"Oh, Lord, I forgot!"

It was some time since they had discussed the independent film Ameropol was bankrolling. Sabrina thought it sounded like fun, but Josh was less enthusiastic. He had gone along with the project, however, and the premiere was set for that evening, with a big party afterward.

"I'll get away as early as I can," she promised.

"We're picking up Simon at seven," Josh pointed out.

Sabrina groaned. Josh knew how much her work meant to her, but Simon still treated it as a hobby she would tire of—the sooner the better, to his way of thinking. It was his first big night out since his illness, and he'd sulk like a two-year-old if she disappointed him.

"Okay, I'll manage somehow," Sabrina sighed.

It was a hectic day. Monsieur Tresante's plane was late, which threw all of her appointments off schedule. By the time she got home that night she was cutting it rather close.

Josh was in the den having a drink and glancing through the paper. He was already dressed in faultlessly tailored evening clothes. The dramatic black and white suited his darkly handsome face and lean, rangy frame. Sabrina took a brief moment to assure him she'd be ready in time before dashing into the bedroom.

She was like a whirling dervish, showering, applying makeup, and dressing in record time. When she joined Josh in the den, Sabrina felt breathless but she looked wonderful. Josh's casual glance turned sultry as he gazed at his wife.

Her sleeveless gown was simply cut, but covered in gold bugle beads from the low neckline to the narrow hem that was eased by a deep slit up one side. The golden shimmer was reflected in the mass of shining blond hair cascading from the crown of her head in a profusion of seemingly unintentional curls.

"I think I'm married to a sorceress," Josh declared. He took her in his arms, kissing the soft skin of her forehead. "I know we're committed to seeing this movie tonight," he whispered, "but I promise you this—we're coming home early!"

Simon was ready and waiting for them, looking very fit in his evening clothes. The weight he had lost was becoming. Beneath the thick thatch of white hair his lean face glowed with health and his blue eyes were clear. They were also annoyed.

"You're seven minutes late," he announced, displaying a handsome gold watch as proof. "If everyone in the world was seven minutes late the wheels of industry would grind to a halt."

"The working day is over," Josh remarked mildly.

"That's no excuse for tardiness. How are you, my dear? You look beautiful as always." Simon kissed Sabrina on the cheek.

"Count your blessings, Grandfather," she remarked demurely. "You're lucky we're here at all."

"Why, what happened?" he demanded, frowning.

"Josh thought of something even more interesting to do tonight, and if you don't stop bellowing at us I'm going to take him up on it."

Simon chuckled, putting an arm around each of them. "You can restrain yourselves for a few hours to make a lonely old man happy."

"You're about as lonely as a drum major in a Fourth of July parade," Josh told him cynically. "And I pity anyone else who called you old."

"Don't you forget it either," Simon agreed cheerfully. "Come on, children, let's go to the party. Those doctors have kept me on the shelf long enough."

As they were walking toward the door, the phone started to ring. "Don't answer it," Sabrina advised.

"I have to see who it is. It might be important." Simon started across the hall.

"You'll start talking business and we'll miss the beginning of the movie," Sabrina warned.

"Nonsense. I'll be with you in a jiffy." Suddenly, being seven minutes late didn't concern Simon any more.

He disappeared into the den, reappearing in the doorway a few moments later to beckon to Josh. After tapping her foot in the hall for a short time, Sabrina went into the den, angry that she had rushed so much only to be standing around waiting now.

The scene that greeted her was about what she expected. Simon's eyes were intent as he barked questions into the phone while Josh leaned over the desk, scribbling figures on a pad of yellow paper. They had forgotten her completely in their total absorption with some pressing problem.

Sighing deeply, Sabrina approached Josh and held out her hand. "Give me my ticket."

He brought his attention back to her with an effort. "This is a trans-Atlantic phone call, honey. It's something we have to take care of."

"I know. Just give me my ticket and try to make it before the end of the movie."

He frowned. "I don't want you going by yourself. We'll be through here as soon as possible."

"Listen to me, Josh Winchester! I didn't hurry home

and get all dressed up just to sit here and watch you and Grandfather conduct business halfway around the world."

"Sit down and be quiet, Sabrina," Simon ordered, looking up in annoyance. "Josh and I are busy."

She looked mockingly at her husband. "When the crisis is over, tell him I've grown up."

Sabrina stepped from the taxi into a scene of frenetic activity. Giant lights slashed the night sky, also lighting up the crowds of people milling around the forecourt of the theater. Long black limousines were disgorging beautifully dressed men and women who stopped to say a few words into a microphone while turning their best profile toward the popping flash bulbs. It was a premiere in the old Hollywood tradition.

On her way to the entrance Sabrina met two old friends, Tricia and Raymond Turner. After chatting a few moments they asked about Josh.

"He and Simon were deep in a business deal when I left them," Sabrina explained. "I'm not sure they'll make the film *or* the party after."

"You can come with us," Tricia offered.

"If things go the way I expect, I might take you up on it."

As Sabrina predicted, the seats on either side of her remained empty. The movie was moderately entertaining, but her resentment grew as it progressed. If she had given up her evening, the least they could do was the same.

By the time the film was over, Sabrina was thoroughly annoyed. If she had entertained any thought of going home directly after the performance, her mind was changed. Sabrina met her friends in the lobby as they'd instructed.

The party was held in the ballroom of a fashionable hotel nearby. It was supposed to be restricted to people connected with the film in some way, but from the looks of the overflow crowd, that included half of Los Angeles. Sabrina began to regret her decision almost immediately. It was hot and noisy, she didn't know anyone there, and she had gotten separated from her friends.

As she was wondering how to find Tricia and Ray to tell them she was leaving, a man's voice behind her said, "Don't tell me a beautiful little doll like you is all alone?"

"Okay, I won't tell you," she muttered. That's all she needed to top off the evening, an unimaginative pickup artist. She turned to confront a man who had played a minor part in the movie. "You're Derek Devlin," she said, adding politely, "I enjoyed your performance."

Actually, he hadn't been very good but Sabrina was brought up to be tactful. Derek Devlin was older than he looked on the screen. The bright lights of the ballroom showed up tiny wrinkles around his eyes. He was also very Hollywood, with carefully styled blond hair and a pale-blue dinner jacket piped in black instead of the more traditional evening clothes.

He answered her compliment with a grin that showed evenly capped teeth. "You'll never make an actor unhappy that way. Why don't we try and find a quiet corner so you can tell me more? Unless some big bruiser is going to show up and try to rearrange my classic features."

"No, I was just leaving. I was waiting for my grandfather and—"

"Your grandfather!" Derek hooted. "Is that what the old sugar daddies are calling themselves these days?"

"I don't know how Simon would feel about being called a sugar daddy," Sabrina observed dryly, "but I wouldn't advise you to call him old—not to his face anyway."

"Simple Simon needn't be touchy about his age." Derek's eyes were on the diamond necklace around Sabrina's slender throat. "He must be quite a guy to get a gorgeous girl like you."

Her lips twitched. "I'm completely devoted to him."

"He must know that or he wouldn't let you go out on the town alone. Where is he tonight?" Derek's probing was tentative as he tried to discover just how devoted Sabrina was.

"On the phone the last time I saw him." Her soft mouth thinned with impatience. "It wouldn't surprise me a bit if he's still there."

"That's not very fair to you," Derek said more confidently. "If the cat's busy, the mouse has a right to play."

Before Sabrina could answer they were interrupted by a distinguished older man. "Good evening, Sabrina, it's good to see you again. How is your grandfather? He's here, of course."

"Hello, Judge Morrison. No, I'm afraid Simon and Josh are settling a crisis with one of their companies."

"I can't believe Simon Sheffield wouldn't be here tonight looking out for Ameropol's interests," the older man remarked jovially.

Out of the corner of her eye Sabrina could see the shocked look on Derek's face. "I think backing this movie was just a whim on Grandfather's part."

The judge chuckled. "You can always tell the age of a man by the price of his toys. Say hello to Simon, my dear, and tell him we enjoyed the movie."

When the older man moved away Derek said, "You're the granddaughter of *Simon Sheffield?*"

She nodded. "Good old Simple Simon, the sugar daddy himself." Derek was so shaken that it was mischievous to remind him, but Sabrina figured he deserved it.

"I didn't mean to . . . that is, if I'd known . . ." He was almost stuttering with dismay.

76

"Don't worry, I won't tell him." Sabrina grinned. "You're too young to be cut down in your prime."

"I hope you'll let me make it up to you," Derek said earnestly.

"What did you have in mind? A diamond bracelet? A Rolls-Royce?"

"I'm serious, Sabrina. I only came over to talk to you because you looked lonely standing here all by yourself. And then my big, stupid mouth got in the way." He made a rueful face. "In this business you get so used to coming on to every beautiful woman you meet that sometimes you're a little slow to recognize real class."

Sabrina relented. "It's all right, Derek. I could have put you straight sooner, but it was really rather amusing."

Someone passing by bumped into them, almost spilling his champagne on Sabrina. Derek put out his arm to shield her. "This place is a madhouse. Will you go out for a drink with me so I can apologize properly?"

She shook her head. "You didn't let me finish earlier. I was going to tell you that I was waiting for my grandfather *and* my husband. I'm married."

"I know that; I read it in the paper. I wasn't asking for a date, just a chance to make amends." Before she could refuse again Derek said, "A bunch of us are going to that new club that just opened, the Show Boat. Please, Sabrina? I'd like to know that there are no hard feelings."

She had heard of the place. It was the new "in" spot frequented by celebrities, and she had heard it was a lot of fun. Sabrina was sorely tempted. Josh would probably be furious but he didn't have any right to be, she told herself. The whole night had been a washout, and it was all his fault! She was certainly entitled to salvage something out of the evening.

Still, she hesitated. "I'm sure you must be here with a date."

77

"Not really a date, just a little starlet the studio asked me to bring. As a matter of fact, there's a guy here who's dying to take over. Just give me a minute to have a word with her and I'll be right back." He hurried off before Sabrina had a chance to object.

She watched Derek approach a tall, curvy brunette with a sulky mouth and too much eye makeup. His first words seemed to provoke an argument. Derek's back was turned but the woman's face was clearly furious. She appeared to have quite a lot to say on the matter.

By the time Derek returned Sabrina had made up her mind. "I'm afraid this isn't a very good idea, Derek. Your friend considers you her date even if you don't. She seemed very put out."

"Tanya? She wasn't angry with me. She was telling me about some producer who promised her a part in his next picture and just told her it fell through. Tough, but those are the breaks." He took Sabrina's arm, steering her toward one of the exits.

It was all just a little too pat. Sabrina stopped at the door. "I considered going with you, Derek, because it's too hot and crowded here and you mentioned that a group of other people were going. I don't know why *you* asked *me* but I can guess. So to save both of us a lot of unpleasantness, I'm going to say good-bye here."

He looked crestfallen. "I don't blame you for being suspicious after the way I acted, Sabrina. I really wanted to get to know you, but I'll take you straight home if you'd rather. Or I'll call you a cab," he added hastily.

Sabrina had the uncomfortable feeling that she had overreacted. "I didn't mean to be rude, Derek. I just didn't want there to be any misunderstandings between us."

Hope returned to his face. "If you'll come with me I'll sit across the table from you—no, I'll sit across the room and send you messages on paper airplanes."

78

Sabrina laughed. "That won't be necessary. If you get out of line I'll just tell Grandfather what you said about him."

Derek was abruptly serious. "Please don't do that, Sabrina!" he said urgently.

"Don't be silly, I was only joking."

She gazed at him thoughtfully. There was no doubt about Derek's apprehension. What on earth did he think Simon could do to him? Since it wasn't important she dismissed the whole thing from her mind.

CHAPTER FIVE

When they arrived at the nightclub, Sabrina found that Derek hadn't been lying to her. A group of his friends were already assembled around a large table. They were all in the entertainment industry, mostly actors, although there were a sprinkling of technicians. Some of the faces were vaguely familiar to Sabrina, but none were big names. They were flamboyant yet fun.

The Show Boat was much like its patrons—gaudy, fast paced, and amusing. The entertainment consisted of improvisation by standup comics. One comedian was especially good. After the show Sabrina commented on it to Derek.

"I wish Josh could have been here." She was unaware of the wistfulness in her voice.

"I'm sorry I'm not as entertaining," Derek said lightly.

She had heard how fragile an actor's ego was. "I didn't mean it that way. I was only wishing that Josh could have heard that last performer. He was really good."

Derek nodded. "And still he's doing improv work for peanuts. This is a tough business. Unless you're a star, it's a chancy way to make a living."

"I've always wondered why so many people stayed in it. To chase a rainbow all your life must be very frustrating."

Derek's smile was twisted. "There's always the chance of catching up to the pot of gold. Just one big break and you're sitting on top of the world, laughing at all the little guys trying to climb the ladder."

It wasn't the noblest way of putting it, Sabrina thought with slight distaste. "You don't seem to be having too many problems. That was quite a good part you had in the film tonight."

"I'm sorry your grandfather wasn't there to see it. Do you think he'll like it?"

"Simon only looks at the bottom line. The picture could win an Academy Award, but if it doesn't make money he'd take it as a personal affront."

"And if it does make money?"

Sabrina laughed. "He'd probably buy a movie studio."

Derek looked stunned. "That's interesting," he murmured.

"Of course he and Josh would have a pitched battle over it."

"Your husband doesn't like the movie industry?"

That was putting it mildly. Josh's opinion of actors didn't bear repeating. "Grownups playing make-believe so they wouldn't have to face reality" was one of the pleasanter ones.

"I think he feels more comfortable in the world of finance," she answered diplomatically.

"There are plenty of money men in the industry. They're the real stars." For a moment Derek's face wore an envious frown.

"It's not the same thing. I've always thought acting looked like fun."

"It is. Have you ever seen a movie being shot?"

"No."

"I'm doing a television show next. It's even better than a movie in a way, because everything is speeded up. Would you like to visit the set?"

"I'd love to but I'm a working woman."

Derek's eyebrows shot up. "What do you do?"

"I'm an associate editor on *La Vie* magazine," Sabrina said proudly.

"I didn't know Ameropol owned magazines too." He shook his head. "Boy, they're into everything."

Sabrina was intensely annoyed. "Ameropol doesn't own *La Vie,*" she said crisply. "My relationship to Simon had nothing to do with my landing this job."

Her displeasure wasn't lost on Derek. "I didn't mean to put you down. I just thought . . ."

"That's all right." She sighed. "It's what everybody thinks."

"Well, it is kind of unusual," he excused himself. "Women like you mostly serve on committees, things like that."

"And read French novels and eat bonbons?" Sabrina smiled grimly at the stereotype. "Sorry to ruin my image, but I work regular hours. As a matter of fact, I have an early-morning appointment tomorrow." She looked at her watch and gasped. "How did it get to be so late? I've got to run! Would you get me a taxi, Derek?"

"Wouldn't think of it. I'll take you home."

"It really isn't necessary."

"Even actors know enough to see a lady to her door," Derek chided. He took a pen out of his breast pocket and scribbled on a cocktail napkin. "This is my phone number if you change your mind about visiting the set—maybe on your lunch hour. Or who knows? Maybe your husband will get another trans-Atlantic phone call and you'll be stuck for an escort at the last minute."

"Are you branching out into a new business?" she joked.

He helped her on with her mink jacket, tucking the cocktail napkin in one of the pockets. "No, you'll be my only client."

82

On the drive home Sabrina said, "I really enjoyed tonight, Derek. You salvaged my evening."

"I'm glad, because you made mine. I hope I can see you again, Sabrina."

"I'm sure you know the answer to that," she replied, hoping he wasn't going to prove difficult.

"I don't mean a date—just lunch sometime. Or perhaps dinner if your husband is tied up and you're feeling at loose ends."

"How is that different from a date?"

"Because we both know there won't be anything involved except conversation. In this day and age, can't a man and a woman be friends?"

"I suppose so," she answered slowly.

"Good, then that's what we'll be. You can tell me how much flack you have to take at the office and I'll tell you what an idiot my director is. How about it?" When she hesitated, searching for a kind way to tell him she wasn't interested, Derek said urgently, "Just consider this the start of a fine friendship."

The car slid to a stop in front of her door, saving Sabrina the necessity of a reply. She slid out quickly but Derek came around to walk her up the path.

When they were standing in front of her door he said, "It was a great evening." He grinned suddenly. "If the picture is a hit, tell your grandfather that I was the one responsible."

Her laughter rippled in the quiet night. "And if it's a flop I'll blame it on the star."

"You've got it!" Derek pressed her hand briefly before walking back to the car.

Sabrina let herself into the darkened house, grateful that Josh was asleep. It really was shockingly late. She had just unbuckled one sandal when the entry hall suddenly blazed with light. She looked up in surprise to see Josh standing there like an avenging angel.

"Josh, you startled me! Did I wake you?" He wore only a pair of black satin pajama bottoms so it was a natural assumption.

"Where the hell have you been?" His voice was a low growl, a fitting accompaniment to his blazing eyes.

That was a fine greeting! "Hello to you too," she answered coldly.

"Answer me! Do you know what time it is?"

Her feathery brows drew together in annoyance. "Too late to play twenty questions."

His face was dark with fury as he approached her. "I want to know where you've been and I want to know *now!*"

She had never seen Josh this way. His body was like a steel coil, menacing her with its power. "You know where I was. I went to the premiere and . . . and then on to the party."

"The party was over hours ago—I checked."

"Well, I—I met someone at the party and we went on to that new club, the Show Boat. A whole group of us," she added hurriedly. Her explanation was only making him more furious.

"Exactly whom did you go with? Who brought you home just now?"

"His name is Derek Devlin. He had a part in the movie tonight," she said tentatively.

Josh's hand gripped her chin, jerking her face up to his. "You went out with a *man* tonight?"

Suddenly Sabrina had had enough. She yanked her face away from his paralyzing fingers. "Not the way you're making it sound. And I suggest that we continue this discussion in our room if you don't want Akira and Michiko to think you've suddenly gone crazy."

She swept disdainfully down the hall, painfully aware of Josh following close behind, like a silent, stalking jungle cat. When they were in their bedroom with the door closed, Sabrina threw her purse and jacket on the bed, every movement expressing righteous indignation. But when she started for the dressing room, Josh seized her arm, whirling her around to face him.

"If you think you're going to give me the silent treatment, you're very much mistaken," he grated.

His fingers were biting into her delicate skin, but Sabrina refused to flinch. "You asked a question and I answered it. Now take your hands off me. I'm tired and I want to go to bed."

His topaz eyes glittered. "You waltz in here at two thirty in the morning, announce that you've been out with a man, and I'm supposed to ask if you had a good time?"

She raised her chin defiantly. "As a matter of fact, I did." Then her eyes grew serious, questioning. "I don't know why you're carrying on like a madman. If you'd been where you were supposed to be tonight, none of this would have happened."

"And what exactly did happen? What were you doing all this time?"

She stared up at him, her own anger fading into incredulity. "Surely you don't think I was with a man, Josh? I mean not that way."

"What else am I supposed to think?" he asked tautly. "I heard you outside the door, laughing together."

She framed his face in her palms. "Look at me, Josh. Do you honestly think I'd let another man touch me?"

He searched her face, his anger draining away. A deep groan wrenched his big frame as he gathered her in a fierce hug. "I was so worried about you! I was just about to call the police and every hospital in town. I kept picturing you —" He buried his face in her hair.

Sabrina was smitten with remorse. She had known Josh would be annoyed, and she figured it served him right. It had never occurred to her that he would be this worried. "I'm sorry, darling. When you and Grandfather didn't show up I knew your business deal had lasted for hours. I thought you'd decided to skip the whole thing and go home to bed."

"It *was* late when we got through," he replied. "I waited for you at home though." He nuzzled the soft hair at her temple. "I wanted to make it up to you."

"You admit I had reason to be annoyed?"

"Yes, but I never thought you'd take this kind of revenge," he said reproachfully.

"I didn't, Josh, not on purpose. It's just that the whole evening was such a washout." She rested her head on his shoulder. "It wasn't any fun without you."

"So you decided to prolong it?" he asked dryly, but his fingers were now caressing the nape of her neck.

"Maybe unconsciously I was trying to teach you a lesson, but I never meant for you to be hurt."

His arms tightened. "I almost went out of my mind! I couldn't live if anything happened to you. Don't ever leave me, sweetheart."

She rubbed her cheek against his shoulder, glorying in the feel of muscle under smooth warm skin. "I tried that once and it didn't work."

"Do you know how lonely it was in that bed?" he demanded. "I kept waiting for you to come home, thinking of all the ways I was going to make love to you."

Sabrina put her arms around his neck, resting her forehead against his so that the tips of their noses touched. "Don't tell me there's a way you haven't thought of yet," she teased.

"You inspire me." Josh's whipcord muscles had relaxed,

but as he ran his hands down her back, guiding her hips to his, she could feel his body tense for a different reason.

She ruffled his dark hair lovingly. "I can't wait to hear about it."

He slid her zipper down very slowly, smiling at her with the tawny eyes of a lion. "There isn't going to be much dialogue."

Slipping the dress off her shoulders, he let it slither down to lie in a shimmering circle on the floor. All she had on under it was a pair of sheer-to-the-waist pantyhose. As Josh's smoky eyes traveled the length of her body, Sabrina began to turn liquid inside.

"Have I told you that you have the most beautiful breasts in the world?" he asked huskily.

His fingertips feathered over them, tracing their fullness before lightly touching the hardening tips. The teasing contact made her gasp with pleasure, and when he circled each nipple with his tongue, Sabrina clutched at his shoulders.

Josh sank to his knees, kissing the soft skin of her stomach while his fingers slipped inside the waistband of her pantyhose, easing them down her hips. He drew them off slowly, pausing to bestow inflaming kisses that drove her wild with desire. When he started the return journey upward, she cried out with delight.

He stood up, swinging her nude body into his arms and holding her against his bare chest. The dark, curling hair was unbelievably sensuous against her naked breasts. She pressed closer to him, murmuring his name.

"You want me, don't you, darling?" he asked exultantly.

"So much," she breathed, closing her eyes to savor the exquisite feeling.

He carried her over to the bed. Sitting on the edge with Sabrina in his arms, Josh stroked her body from shoulder to thigh, lingering over every erotic spot. "Do you know what it feels like to have you flame like this in my arms?" He groaned.

"Love me, Josh!" It was a primitive command that wouldn't be denied.

She pushed him backward onto the bed, pulling his pajama bottoms off then swiftly covering his body with hers. As her legs parted, Sabrina's mouth sought Josh's. His tongue engaged hers eagerly, his urgency rising to meet hers. Cupping his hands around her hips, he completed their union.

His driving force carried her higher and higher, each new spiral more pulsating than the one before. The intoxicating climb peaked suddenly in a burst of sensation that engulfed them completely. The thunderous waves that crashed through her body subsided gradually, leaving a gentle, throbbing release.

After a long while Josh rolled her over in his arms, twining his legs around hers. He fitted her body to the curve of his, resting his head on her breast. "Have I told you I love you, Mrs. Winchester?" he asked sleepily.

"Not in the last hour, but it's all right." She snuggled closer, stroking his hair with languid pleasure. "Actions do speak louder than words."

After that night, life was even more wonderful. The depth of Josh's feeling for her filled Sabrina with inexpressible joy. His concern when he thought something might have happened to her took care of any lingering doubts. Josh loved her as totally as she loved him!

Everything was fulfilling at work too. Sabrina was beginning to get recognition for her efforts. Not long after the premiere she was called into the editor-in-chief's office. The raise she received was accompanied by a nice speech commending her work.

Sabrina walked on air back to her own office. Her first

impulse was to call Josh to share the news, but she decided against it. This triumph deserved a celebration. She would have Josh take her somewhere very posh for lunch and tell him over champagne cocktails.

The decision was hard to keep. Sabrina was bursting with impatience long before lunchtime. When the hour finally arrived she sped up Wilshire Boulevard, thankful that the Ameropol building was within walking distance. Her spirits were high as she headed toward Josh's office on the top floor.

When Sabrina eagerly entered the reception area she found Mrs. Grayling, Josh's secretary, talking to a tall brunette. "Hello, Mrs. Winchester! How nice to see you again." Mrs. Grayling could never be accused of being unenthusiastic. "Is Mr. Winchester expecting you?"

Before Sabrina could reply, the door to Josh's inner office opened. "I thought I heard a familiar name." He went over to give Sabrina a brief, conventional kiss on the mouth. "To what do I owe the honor of this visit?"

There was something unsatisfying about the brief little peck, although she understood the necessity for it. "I thought you might take me to lunch," she said.

"It's a distinct possibility. Come in my office and we'll discuss the matter." As the brunette started for the outer door, Josh said, "Did you want to see me, Diane?"

"I did, but it can wait till you get back from lunch."

"I can spare a few minutes," he said.

"I have an appointment at two," Sabrina told him.

"These figures will wait," Diane assured Josh.

He frowned slightly, noticing the thick sheaf of papers in her hand. "What figures are those?"

"I have the results of our advertising campaign."

Josh's face was suddenly intent. It bore the look he always wore when he was facing a business challenge. "Are they favorable?"

89

"For the most part," Diane answered. "There's one gray area, but I think I know what the trouble is."

"Let's go into my office," he said decisively.

"It isn't anything urgent," she protested. "Take your wife to lunch. I'll give you my report this afternoon."

"This will only take a minute. I want to have a quick look at those sales figures."

Diane shrugged, giving Sabrina a rueful look. As Sabrina followed them into Josh's office, her temper started to rise. She didn't blame Diane. The other woman had assured him that the matter could wait. It was Josh who didn't let anything stand in the way of business—not even his wife.

Sabrina stood at the wide windows, looking at the view that spread all the way to downtown on one side and to the far mountains on the other. It was a panorama that usually enthralled her, but not that day. After fifteen minutes she turned to stare at Josh and Diane, their heads close together, poring over the closely typed sheets. They were both completely engrossed. Sabrina looked at her watch. With the time spent getting to Josh's office and now this, more than half an hour was gone from her lunch period.

"Josh, I'm going to have to be getting back soon," she called sharply.

"In a minute, honey," he answered absently.

She left the window to stand over him. "I won't have time for lunch if we don't leave right now." Even so, her plans for an elegant restaurant would have to be scrapped.

He continued to scribble numbers on a pad of yellow paper. "I'm sure they won't fire you if you're a little late."

A wave of fury swept over Sabrina. The colossal, unmitigated gall of him! His position was important but hers wasn't. He was showing what he thought of her job *and* her! Sabrina was too angry to trust herself to answer. She walked stiffly to the door, closing it softly behind her.

Her hands were clenched into fists as she went down the hall to the elevator. Sabrina was so preoccupied that she almost didn't hear her name called.

"What a nice surprise, darling." Simon caught up with her and kissed her cheek. "What are you doing here?"

"I was just leaving." She tried to compose herself.

"Without stopping to say hello to your only living grandfather? Outrageous! Have you had lunch yet?"

"No, I was going to—I mean, I have to get back."

"You have to eat." He rang for the elevator. "Come on, I'll take you someplace scandalously expensive." He winked at her. "I know the man who okays the expense accounts."

The last thing Sabrina wanted was to have lunch with her grandfather. He had an uncanny way of sensing when something was bothering her. "I'd love to, but I simply don't have time."

"Okay, I'll give you a raincheck." As she sighed with relief Simon took her arm, piloting her into the elevator, which arrived at that moment. "We'll just go downstairs to the coffee shop."

She knew it was useless to refuse. Minutes later, as she settled into the leather booth next to him, Sabrina concentrated on suppressing her feelings.

"What have you and Josh been doing with yourselves?" Simon asked after the waitress had left them alone with menus. "I never see you any more."

"You see Josh every day," she pointed out.

"But not you, and you're prettier." He covered her hand with his, suddenly becoming serious. "You don't know what it means to me to see you settled down and happy." When her eyes flickered away from his, he asked sharply, "You *are* happy, aren't you, Sabrina?"

"Wildly." She smiled gamely.

He looked at her searchingly. "Why do I get the feeling that you're not telling me the truth?"

"Oh, Grandfather, don't be silly! What could be wrong?"

"That's what I'm trying to find out. Have you and Josh been arguing again?"

"First you have to get his attention," she replied grimly.

"What is that supposed to mean?"

"Nothing! I—I'm just a little jumpy today." She glanced at her watch. "I have an appointment at two so we'd better order." She made a great show of looking at the menu, but he didn't open his.

"It's that job of yours," Simon decided. "You're working too hard for no good reason. It's all a lot of damn foolishness."

Even though she knew nothing was going to change her grandfather's thinking at his age, Sabrina couldn't repress her irritation. "It's a whole different world out there now. Women don't stay home anymore, worrying about how to get the family wash cleaner than white. They're fully entrenched in the business world."

"I don't want to know what women are doing, you're the one I'm concerned with. You ought to be at home starting a family."

"In the middle of the day?" It was a weak attempt but the subject was unwelcome in her present mood.

"Don't be flip with me, young lady. I'd like to be a great-grandfather before I'm too old to enjoy the little nipper. And Josh isn't getting any younger either. I'll bet he agrees with me, doesn't he?"

"I don't know, we've never discussed it," Sabrina replied coolly.

"What is there to discuss? Conversation doesn't play a large part in it," he remarked dryly.

She straightened her fork with great deliberation. "Maybe Josh doesn't want children."

"*Maybe!* Do you mean you don't know? I swear to heaven, you two communicate less than any two people I ever met. If it was left to the pair of you, you wouldn't even be married now!"

Sabrina became very still as his words seemed to echo loudly in the awkward silence that ensued. And yet, hadn't she always suspected it without wanting to believe it was so? "You tricked me into marrying Josh, didn't you?" she asked quietly.

Simon looked uncomfortable. His easily ignitible temper had clearly betrayed him. He tried to cover it up with bluster. "I have no idea what you're talking about. Order your lunch!"

"When you couldn't get your own way you used blackmail," she said slowly, almost to herself. "That whole deathbed scene was an act."

"I'm sorry if I disappointed you by not dying," he answered austerely.

Sabrina felt as though a huge weight had settled on her chest. "There's only one thing I want to know—was Josh in on it?"

"You're letting your imagination run away with you, child."

"He had to be. That would explain a lot of things," she mused, her eyes narrowing as she remembered the conversation between Josh and her grandfather at the hotel in Amsterdam.

"Well, maybe I did help things along a little," Simon admitted grudgingly. "But what difference does it make now? Everything worked out all right."

"For whom?" Sabrina asked grimly.

"I don't know what's gotten into you. I had only your best interests at heart." Simon was whipping up righteous

93

indignation to assuage his conscience. "You told me yourself that you were very happy. Can you sit there and deny that you're in love with Josh?"

"No," she murmured, dropping her long lashes. Nothing Josh could do would change that. It was a tragedy she'd have to live with.

"Then I don't see what the big deal is. You love him and he loves you. What more could you possibly want?"

Sabrina slid out of the booth to stand over her grandfather, staring down somberly. "For a usually astute man, you have a couple of remarkable blind spots." Squaring her slim shoulders, she turned and walked out of the coffee shop.

CHAPTER SIX

Sabrina walked slowly back to her office, trying to assess all the things that had happened in the last hour. Simon's revelation came under the heading of things she'd rather not have known. She had succeeded in convincing herself that Josh truly loved her. Apparently Simon had played into his hands by engineering their remarriage. Could he be using Simon too and gaining unbounded power right under his very nose?

Josh's deception was appalling. Simon was convinced that Josh loved her. He couldn't conceive of the fact that she might be merely the means to an end. A very palatable means—no one could deny that their sex life was sensational—but it wasn't enough, Sabrina thought rebelliously. She wouldn't be used!

Mercifully, the day was a busy one. Sabrina's two-o'clock appointment ran overtime, making it a rush to keep the rest of her schedule. Then at the close of the day there was a phone call that kept her at her desk.

When she finally got home, Josh was already there. He was in the den fixing a drink. Sabrina would have gone on to the bedroom if he hadn't called to her.

"What happened to you today?" he asked, as though nothing was wrong. "I thought we were going to have lunch."

Sabrina's body was stiff with outrage. "That was the

general idea, but I realize that I can't compete with a sales chart."

One of Josh's dark eyebrows rose. "Don't you think you're being a little unreasonable? I told you I wanted to glance over that report."

"And I told *you* I had a two-o'clock appointment. Besides, you did more than glance. I waited for fifteen minutes."

"Perhaps I did get a little involved," he said mildly. "But we still would have had time for lunch."

"Because it didn't matter if I was late, as you so kindly pointed out." Her eyes glittered like emeralds. "My little job isn't important, only yours."

"I never said that," Josh replied evenly. "I'm enormously proud of your success. I admire your determination as much as your talent."

"Is that why you expected me to break an appointment for the pure pleasure of watching you ignore me?" she asked sarcastically.

His mouth thinned ominously. "I never suggested nor expected that. For one thing, you showed up at my office without calling first to see if I had lunch plans already. And suppose we had a luncheon date and a crisis came up unexpectedly in *your* office. Would you have dropped everything to keep our date?"

"It's not the same thing at all! Your figures weren't a crisis—they could have waited."

"And so could have you."

She lifted her chin and glared at him. "Okay, then let's just say I didn't choose to."

"That's more like it. Now I'd like to know the reason why. The real reason, Sabrina."

"You got what you wanted. You got to see those precious figures. You can't have it all!"

"Why do I get the feeling that we're no longer talking

96

about lunch plans? What is this really all about?" he asked softly.

There was no point in evading the issue. They couldn't go on living a lie. "I met Simon in the hall after I left your office," she said abruptly. "We had lunch together."

"And?" There was something wary about Josh now.

"He told me the truth about our marriage—inadvertently, of course," she added cynically.

"What is the truth?"

"Don't pretend innocence, Josh, I know the whole story —the phone deathbed request, the hurried marriage, the romantic honeymoon in Europe. You and Grandfather planned the whole thing."

"That isn't so," he answered quietly.

"How can you deny it when Grandfather practically admitted it to me? You both knew I'd do anything he asked if I thought he was dying."

Josh hesitated, choosing his words carefully. "I didn't know at first that his relapse was faked. When I started to suspect as much, Simon convinced me that he was doing the right thing. But if you think back, you'll remember that I told him I wouldn't marry you against your will."

"I was too scared to think clearly!" she exclaimed. "How could you have taken advantage of that?"

His strong, capable hands cupped her shoulders as he looked down into her flushed face. "I wanted you back so badly I wasn't willing to question the methods. Simon said you still loved me and I had to take a chance."

"Did you feed him the fiction that *you* still loved *me?*"

"He already knew that." Josh ran his fingers through her silky hair, tucking it in back of one ear in a caressing motion. "By now you must know it too," he said in a husky voice.

Josh had taken off his jacket and removed his tie. His shirt was unbuttoned halfway down his broad chest, and with his cuffs rolled partway up his muscular forearms he was all male, virile and sensual. But for the first time Sabrina didn't react to his blatant masculinity. Josh turned on his charm a little too easily.

She moved a slight distance away. "Aren't you confusing love with desire?" she asked coldly.

"They're the same thing in your case." He closed the gap between them. "I love you and I desire you," he murmured, reaching out to her.

She pushed his hand away. "No, Josh, this time it's not going to work."

The dawning passion drained out of his face as he stared down at her. "I'm sorry that you had to find out in a way that was upsetting, but aren't you overreacting a little? We're together again and we're happy. Isn't that the important thing?"

"You and Simon planned your defense well. The end justifies the means, is that it?"

"I'm not proud of deceiving you," he answered steadily. "But if I'd stood on my ethics, we'd still be divorced."

"And we both know you never let ethics stand in your way when you really want something," she mocked. "Especially such a valuable acquisition."

Josh's eyes narrowed speculatively. "This is more than the fact that we misled you, isn't it, Sabrina? I think you'd better tell me everything that's on your mind."

He was right; she was tired of being played for a fool. Sabrina's hurt and resentment tumbled out. "I know now why you married me—both times. It's a classic textbook route to success—marry the boss's daughter and get rich!"

He looked at her incredulously. "I was rich before I married you."

"But I represent power, the ultimate aphrodisiac. When Simon dies I'll inherit his stock, and you'll control Ameropol."

Josh's eyes blazed with sudden intensity. "Was this why you left me? You used what you thought was another woman only as a convenient excuse?"

Sabrina felt almost calm now that it was all out in the open. "I wasn't exactly thrilled to find out my husband was cheating on me. You might say it was the last straw."

He grabbed her arms in a paralyzing grip. "The fact that I told you I loved you meant nothing? You think all those nights in my arms were faked?"

Her mouth twisted in a self mocking smile. "A man doesn't have to be in love to enjoy sex. That was a fringe benefit that also served to keep me happy."

His hands tightened. "At least you're willing to admit I made you happy."

"It must have amused you greatly to know how little it took," she answered bitterly.

Josh stared at her for a long moment before releasing her. A mask seemed to descend over his face. "That's not very flattering," he drawled. "I thought my lovemaking was quite inspired."

Sabrina felt an actual pain in her chest. It was devastating to hear him practically admit that he had used her, even though she was finally aware of it. Suddenly Sabrina couldn't bear any more.

"There's really no point in discussing it any further," she said in a low voice that she fought to keep steady. "We both know what the truth is."

Josh shrugged. "Okay, so what do we do now?"

She looked at him blankly. It was something she hadn't considered. It was unthinkable that they go on with the charade of their marriage, but the thought of never seeing Josh again was like a knife in her midsection.

His expression was sardonic as he watched the play of emotions over her mobile face. "Another divorce, Sabrina? I can just see the tabloids now. 'Smoking Winchesters pointed at each other again. Sabrina to fire the next round in court.' "

Josh was right of course, the newspapers would have a field day with their brief remarriage. And there wasn't any real hurry about a divorce, she told herself. As long as she and Josh understood each other, why not keep up appearances? She wondered if she was harboring the hope that Josh's desire could turn into love.

"I don't see the necessity for a divorce yet, with all its attendant publicity," she said with dignity. "Let's let things cool down a bit so we'll be acting with level heads."

Josh's face was unreadable. "Let me get this straight. You won't believe that I love you, but you're proposing that we go on living together as though nothing happened?"

"Not exactly," she replied distantly. "I'm suggesting that we pretend to *other* people that nothing's happened. I'm sure we can manage to act civilized whenever it's necessary to appear in public together."

"I see. How about Akira and Michiko? Are they going to be in on our little secret?"

The loyal Japanese couple had been so happy about their reunion. They wouldn't understand this new arrangement at all. "Maybe it would be better if they didn't know."

"In that case we'll have to continue sharing a bedroom. Can we also manage to act civilized there?" Josh asked mockingly.

Furious anger swept through Sabrina. He was so sure of himself! Josh thought she couldn't resist him. That one night in his arms would make all his transgressions seem unimportant. Well, maybe it had been that way in the past, but no more! She would show him that he no longer had any power over her.

"It won't be any problem for me," she remarked coldly.

"Won't it, Sabrina?" His soft voice curled around her like a caress. "Do you honestly think we can sleep in the same bed without making love? It hasn't seemed to work in the past."

"Don't count on my making the same mistake again," she declared tautly. "Even a child learns not to play with fire after she's been burned."

"But you're not a child, Sabrina." His mocking eyes traveled lazily over her body, lingering on the thrust of her breasts under the silk blouse. "You're a lovely, passionate woman."

"Who believes that love is necessary for sex to be fulfilling," she said through clenched teeth. "You needn't worry about my attacking you in the middle of the night."

"You don't love me any more?" He snapped his fingers. "Just like that?"

"I don't *like* you!" she flared. "Because I can't really believe that *you* love *me.* And that's the first step. Now that we understand each other, I'm going to take off my things."

It was one of the worst evenings of Sabrina's life. Michiko had prepared dinner so they had to sit down at the table in the gracious dining room as if it were a normal evening. Since Akira was in and out of the room serving, they were also forced to make idle conversation.

"How was your day?" Josh asked politely.

"Just fine, and yours?"

"Rather unexpected." He slanted her a rueful smile. When she didn't react Josh's smile died. "Anything interesting happen?"

"Not really," she replied indifferently. "Oh yes, one thing—I got a raise."

"That's wonderful!" Sudden comprehension flooded his face. "Is that why you came to have lunch with me?"

She shrugged. "It isn't important."

"But it is." Josh's voice was muted with regret. "I'm sorry, Sabrina. Why didn't you tell me?"

"I was saving it as a surprise. Wasn't that naive of me?" He groaned. "If I'd only known."

The bitterness of her frustrated moment of glory almost choked Sabrina. "It worked out for the best. This way you didn't have to pretend that you considered it important."

"Sabrina!" His eyes were reproachful. "How can I convince you that I know what this must mean to you?"

"You can't," she answered briefly. "Isn't this lime sherbert delicious?" she remarked brightly as Akira came in to serve the coffee.

Dinner was bad enough, but the worst was yet to come. If she and Josh didn't have specific plans for the evening, they usually sat in the den after dinner, talking and listening to music. That night Sabrina decided to go to bed and read.

It was a good idea that had no chance of success. She turned page after page dutifully, not absorbing a single word. Her complete attention was centered on Josh. What was he doing in the other room? Did he intend to join her eventually, or was he going to sleep in the guest room?

When he came into the bedroom a little later, her heart took a giant leap. Sabrina pretended great interest in her book, watching him from under lowered lashes. Josh seemed unaffected by the tension that gripped her. He followed his usual routine, emptying his pockets and putting the contents on the dresser. The only thing that was missing was the casual conversation they ordinarily indulged in.

When he started to get undressed Sabrina stopped watching. She knew all too well what she would see. His lean torso would appear first as he took off his shirt. After sitting down on the padded bench at the foot of the bed, Josh would take off his shoes and socks, then his trousers.

He would fold them neatly over his brass valet before sliding out of his shorts, revealing the taut body she knew so well. Not an ounce of fat blurred his magnificent form.

Sabrina peered through her lashes involuntarily, confirming what she already expected. But when Josh turned toward the bed completely unselfconsciously her breath caught in her throat. Surely he wasn't going to come to bed nude! It was the way they usually slept, but he must realize that things had changed. Didn't he notice that she had worn a nightgown?

The answer to that was obvious. Josh intended to use his body as a weapon. He expected to seduce her, to reduce her to mindless compliance in his arms. The knowledge was a shield. For once in his life, Josh Winchester was going to get his comeuppance!

"Good night," he murmured politely as he slid between the sheets.

"Will the light bother you?" Sabrina asked, equally politely. "I just want to finish this chapter. The book is so fascinating I can't put it down."

"Read as long as you like," Josh said, turning on his side, facing away from her. "I don't think anything could keep me awake tonight. I'm beat."

She forced herself to ignore him, her fingers tightening on the book until her knuckles were white. When, incredibly, his steady breathing told Sabrina that Josh was actually asleep, she was filled by a desolate feeling. His ability to follow a normal routine told her more than words how little she meant to him. Tears sprang to Sabrina's eyes but she stifled them angrily, turning off the light in case Josh should wake up.

She lay stiffly in the darkness, staring up at the ceiling and willing herself not to cry. Maybe the best course after all was to get a divorce. How could she endure the torture of lying next to him night after night? Then it occurred to her that was what Josh was counting on. No, damn it! she told herself angrily. Josh was a very physical man. Let's see how long *he* could stand it. Her satisfaction was short-lived. It occurred to her that he would seek solace outside their bedroom, as he had done once before.

There were circles under Sabrina's eyes the next morning and her body felt a hundred years old. Josh was in the shower so she went out to the breakfast room to have coffee. Normally she would have called a joyous greeting, sometimes accepting his invitation to join him in the shower. That morning she didn't even intend to have breakfast with him.

By the time Josh came out, clean-shaven and handsome in his superbly tailored suit, Sabrina had finished her juice and coffee. Since neither Akira nor Michiko were in the room, she passed him without a word. When she got out of the shower, Josh had left for work.

Sabrina spend a miserable day. Although she'd had ample warning that Josh was following her lead, she couldn't help expecting him to call. Surely he realized that the situation was intolerable! They would simply have to talk about it; they couldn't go on ignoring each other. If only Josh had defended himself, she reflected wistfully. Pushing the futile wish out of her mind, Sabrina started to straighten her cluttered desk. How do you defend the indefensible?

When she got home Josh's red Ferrari was in the circular drive instead of in the garage where he usually parked it unless they were going out. Sabrina bypassed it, putting away her own car. She sat in the car after she had turned off the motor, trying to outguess him. Had Josh made a date for them, just to try her further? Or was he going out on his own? Most probably the latter. She ignored the pain that caused. If that's the way he wanted it, it was fine with her.

Sabrina entered the house with her small chin tilted at a pugnacious angle. After greeting Akira she went into the den, prepared for anything Josh intended dishing out. But he wasn't there.

"Mr. Winchester is packing," Akira informed her helpfully.

Sabrina felt hot and made an effort to speak. She was surprised when her voice sounded normal. "Thank you, Akira." Her legs didn't seem to have any joints as she walked down the hall to the bedroom.

Josh looked up from a suitcase he was filling. "I'm glad you're home, Sabrina. I thought I'd have to leave you a note."

She arranged her frozen lips into a faint smile. "What was it going to say, thanks for the memories?"

His face was enigmatic as he ignored her question. "I have to go to New York. I'm catching the eight-o'clock flight."

The relief was so great that she sagged against the back of a chair. Josh wasn't leaving her! Almost immediately Sabrina realized that he must never know how the possibility affected her.

She walked casually over to the closet, taking off her jacket. "Business or pleasure?" she asked in a disinterested tone.

He smiled sardonically. "Business, naturally. Isn't that my grand passion?"

Sabrina reached for a hanger, keeping her back turned. "I'm sure you'll find time for a few others."

"If you say so." Josh's voice was as offhand as hers.

"Are you . . . when are you coming home?"

"I'm not sure. I'll let you know." He looked at Sabrina without seeing her as he went through a mental checklist. Making up his mind that he'd remembered everything, Josh snapped his luggage shut. "I'll be at the Plaza if you need me." He paused at the door, raising a mocking eyebrow. "Although I'm sure the need won't arise."

Sabrina stared at the door long after he had gone. What was really behind this sudden business trip? Was it truly necessary, or did Josh have an ulterior motive? Was she supposed to miss him so much that all would be forgiven when he returned? It was sickening to have to try to figure out what plot her own husband was hatching. They were like two adversaries playing high-stakes poker—except that this was no game.

The following day was the Japanese couple's day off. They wanted to forego it since Josh was out of town, but Sabrina wouldn't hear of it.

"I don't like to leave you here all alone in this big house," Michiko protested.

"I'll be perfectly all right. I have a lot of personal things to do," Sabrina assured her.

"Well . . . if you're sure. When will Mr. Winchester be home?"

"I forgot to ask him," Sabrina replied smoothly, as though it were the most natural thing in the world not to care how long your husband was gone. "He'll probably call tonight to tell me."

It was a long day and an even longer night. At least she was busy at the office, but when Sabrina returned to the empty house, the evening stretched ahead interminably. It was so terribly quiet. The beautiful modern home was set well back for privacy, with tall trees ringing the property line. There weren't even any traffic noises to break the stillness.

After changing into a white silk caftan printed with exotic black flowers, she went into the kitchen. A brief glance into the well-stocked refrigerator showed that Michiko had prepared a casserole for her dinner. There was also a fruit salad neatly wrapped in plastic and a chocolate dessert in a crystal parfait glass. It all looked very appetizing, but Sabrina decided she wasn't hungry.

She wandered into the den and turned the television on to the news. It was almost as depressing as her frame of mind. When the program was over a comedy show came on that was so silly she switched it off after a few minutes. Then she tried reading a book.

By nine o'clock Sabrina faced the fact that Josh wasn't going to phone. It was midnight in New York. On previous business trips he had called her every night, sometimes more than once—before he went to dinner and again to say good night. It didn't matter that things had changed drastically between them. The very least he could do would be to let her know when to expect him back. Or was she supposed to go ahead and make plans without him?

Latent anger began to run through her like a current. Wherever Josh was at this moment, she was sure that he wasn't alone. Josh was neither sitting by the phone nor agonizing over what to do about their marriage. By his callous indifference he was telling her to do whatever she wanted. Now that it was all out in the open, he wasn't bothering to play the attentive husband.

Sabrina paced up and down the den floor, crossing her arms tightly to her. Did Josh plan on taking a lot of these trips? Was it his solution to their problem? In that case she was going to have to make a life for herself. She was never going to spend another evening like this one, Sabrina decided fiercely.

The logistics of it were a little tricky. If they were going to keep up appearances, she could hardly go out on dates with other men. It would also be difficult to see her women friends repeatedly without including their respective husbands. There must be someone at loose ends like herself someone she could share an evening with as a friend.

The word stirred something in her memory. Sabrina

107

stopped pacing. Derek Devlin! He had offered her exactly the kind of friendship she was looking for. She had never expected to take him up on it, but his phone number was still in the pocket of her white mink jacket. She hadn't worn it since that night.

Without giving herself time to think about it, Sabrina went in the bedroom and extracted the crumpled cocktail napkin. There was always the chance that Derek's suggestion of a friendly dinner was just a line—Sabrina wasn't naive. But what did she have to lose? Knowing that Simon was her grandfather, he wasn't going to be *that* difficult, and at least she wouldn't have to go through another night like this one.

Sabrina was very embarrassed when a woman answered Derek's phone. Her eyes went to the clock—it was almost ten. It hadn't occurred to her that he might not be alone.

She almost hung up when the woman asked sharply, "Who is this?"

Derek's voice in the background echoed the question. "Who is it?"

When Sabrina quietly asked for Derek, the woman didn't even respond. "Some girl for you." She seemed to be handing the receiver to Derek. "I'd like to know who it is too. Do you have friends I don't know about?"

He didn't bother to answer her, but his voice showed that he was annoyed. "Hello. Derek Devlin here." The curt greeting wasn't promising.

Sabrina gave her name, wishing she'd had sense enough to hang up. The ultimate humiliation would be if he didn't remember her. "We met at the premiere of your new picture," she added, wondering what excuse she could give for calling—since she had decided against the real one.

"Sabrina! How fantastic to hear from you." The transformation was dramatic. Derek's voice was warm and welcoming, all traces of surliness gone.

Sabrina breathed a sigh of relief, but the slightly awkward moment had definitely changed her mind. "I'm sorry to have bothered you, Derek. I didn't realize it was this late."

"It's the shank of the evening, and you aren't bothering me."

"You have company, I won't keep you."

"No, I don't—not the way you mean. My sister is visiting from Chicago."

"I see." Sabrina didn't believe it for a minute.

Her doubt must have shown because Derek chuckled. "She's a good kid but she likes to know who all my friends are so she can report back to her canasta group. I'm afraid little sister is star struck." At an angry exclamation in the background, Derek said, "It's true, Sis." He returned to Sabrina, dismissing the matter. "I'm glad you phoned. It gives me another chance to tell you how much I enjoyed our evening together."

"I did too, Derek. That's why I called, to thank you." He had given her the perfect excuse.

There was disappointment in his voice. "I thought maybe you were going to take me up on that lunch offer."

"As I told you, I'm a working woman," she answered lightly.

"And I suppose dinner is out of the question." Before she could agree he asked, "How did your grandfather like the movie?"

They had never discussed it, but she couldn't tell Derek that. It was the paramount thing in his life. "He seemed quite pleased," she said, wondering if that were true.

"And your husband? Did he change his mind about show biz?"

"I wouldn't know." Sabrina immediately regretted the coldness in her voice. She tried to cover it. "Josh has been so busy lately. I don't even know if he's seen the film."

"Maybe you could ask him and let me know." Derek gave a rueful laugh. "I don't mean to sound pushy, but it means an awful lot to me."

"Well, it may be awhile before I can give you a report. Josh is in New York right now."

"Oh?" There was a world of innuendo in the small word. After a moment's pause Derek remarked, "That must be a real bummer for you, being all alone."

"I don't mind. I manage to keep busy."

"I'm sure you do, with the number of friends you have. Was this one of the evenings you stayed home to rest up?"

Sabrina stiffened, examining his question for sarcasm, but there didn't seem to be any. He sounded interested and respectful. Sabrina knew that Derek was as celebrity struck as his sister, in a different way. He thought corporate people led glamorous lives in keeping with their money. Bitter laughter rose in her throat as she thought of the evening she'd just spent.

"Yes, I really had to stay home tonight and catch up on things," she told him.

"Isn't there any chance that we can have dinner, Sabrina?" Derek asked wistfully.

It was the reason she had called. What was holding her back? A silly misunderstanding over his sister? Derek wouldn't be talking that openly if it weren't true. Sabrina decided to take the plunge—but cautiously.

"I only have tomorrow night open, and I'm sure you're not free on such short notice," she said carelessly.

"For you I'll *be* free."

"I wouldn't want you to break another date."

"I'd do a lot more than that for the chance to see you again."

Sabrina was ready to back out again. "Derek, I don't want you to expect—"

"Relax, honey. I said there wouldn't be anything in-

110

volved but conversation, and I meant it. Suppose I pick you up tomorrow night at seven. Will that give you enough time to get home?"

She thought swiftly. Akira and Michiko would be there and she didn't see how she could explain it to them. "I never know when I'll get held up at the office. Why don't I just meet you at the restaurant?"

If Derek thought that was contrived he didn't show it. "Sounds fine. How about the Fern Grotto? And don't worry if you're late."

After Sabrina hung up she felt exhilarated. It wasn't the prospect of seeing Derek again, it was her own emancipation she was celebrating. If Josh thought she was going to sit home like a sad Cinderella, he was going to find out differently!

The realization of how far they were drifting apart was a sudden, hurtful thought, but she forced it down resolutely.

CHAPTER SEVEN

Sabrina no longer jumped expectantly every time the phone rang. Which was sensible, because Josh didn't call her at the office the next day either. For once things were a little less hectic and she was able to get off on time.

Once she got home, she began to plan her ensemble. The dress she chose was a white two-piece silk. The slim skirt was topped by a simple long-sleeved tunic with a high round neck. She bypassed the diamond necklace in its blue velvet case, selecting instead a beautiful carved jade pendant on a thin gold chain. It had been a gift from Simon, not Josh.

Sabrina had told Michiko that morning that she would be out for dinner. As she prepared to leave, the housekeeper came out of the kitchen.

"You look just lovely, Mrs. Winchester."

"Thanks, Michiko. I'll see you later." She was at the door when the other woman stopped her.

"If Mr. Winchester calls, where shall I tell him you've gone?"

Sabrina's fingers tightened around the knob. "I won't be where he can reach me. Don't worry though, I don't expect him to phone." She left quickly before the housekeeper could ask any more questions.

Derek was waiting when she got to the restaurant. He

looked at her with glowing eyes. "You're here! I kept telling myself you were going to stand me up."

"Am I late?" Sabrina glanced at her watch.

"No, but you don't know how I've been looking forward to this evening."

"Don't tell me you're that hard up for conversation," she remarked coolly, sliding gracefully into the chair he held for her.

Derek laughed. "Okay, I get the message—no compliments. You're a very suspicious lady. All I'm trying to say is that I'm happy to be with you."

"Why, Derek?" She gave him a level look. "Most men in your industry wouldn't consider spending an evening like this. One without any possibility of . . . a payoff. Why did you ask me out?"

A little smile lingered around his mouth. "There's more than one kind of payoff."

"What do you mean?" she inquired sharply.

"You're a very beautiful woman, Sabrina. I like being seen with you. But I'll admit that's not the whole reason." He stared at her searchingly, examining her hairdo, the jade pendant around her neck, the way one graceful hand was resting on the table. "I've never known anyone like you. You come from a world I've only glimpsed."

"I could say that about you too."

"It isn't the same thing. I've played millionaires in movies, but I could never really get into the part. I don't know how they feel about things, how they react."

"F. Scott Fitzgerald notwithstanding, the rich are like anyone else, they just have more money," Sabrina remarked lightly.

"It's more than money. It's education and upbringing. It gives you an advantage the rest of us don't have."

"Anyone can get an education," Sabrina observed. "All

113

you have to do is work for it. Even the rich have to do that."

He shook his head. "You still don't get what I'm driving at. I saw a picture of your husband once. You could look at him and tell that he was somebody, you can tell he went to Harvard."

"Yale," she murmured.

"It's the same thing," Derek said impatiently.

Sabrina smiled. "I don't think either school would thank you for that."

He barely heard her. Derek was frowning, his face intent. "There's a kind of self-confidence about you people that the rest of us don't have."

"Are you trying to say that you asked me out tonight because I'm a member of the monied class? It isn't contagious," she commented dryly.

"I'm hoping some of it will rub off on me. The culture," he added hastily.

Sabrina stared at him in surprise. Derek had seemed so assured when she was with him. "I can't see any lack in you," she said slowly. "Your manners are good, your clothes are attractive, you seem to frequent all the best places."

"Put me up against your husband and I'd look like a bum," Derek stated bluntly.

Sabrina's fingers clenched a spoon as Josh's image suddenly arose in her mind, the confident set of his broad shoulders, the straightforward way he had of looking at everyone with those all-seeing topaz eyes that changed color with his moods. Not very many men could measure up to Josh, but she couldn't very well confirm Derek's judgment.

"I wouldn't say that," she murmured.

"I just said it for you. Sharks like Josh Winchester and Simon Sheffield control the destiny of little fish like me."

114

It wasn't only *his* destiny they held power over. Both men had tried to manipulate her for their own ends. "Nobody can control you if you don't let them," she said sharply.

Derek's smile was twisted. "That just shows how big a gap there is between us—like the distance between Los Angeles and Beverly Hills. Most people think Beverly Hills is a suburb of L.A. They don't know it's really a private enclave. But ask the people who live across the tracks. You can bet your little booties *they* know!"

Sabrina was puzzled at the passion he was displaying. "You can't blame someone for the accident of their birth."

"Is that what you think I'm doing?" He looked at her incredulously. "Baby, I'm not blaming you. I just want to join the club!"

"I don't see—" she began helplessly.

"You were brought up by your grandfather, weren't you?" he digressed abruptly.

"Practically. I was ten when I came to live with him."

"I grew up here too. My mother was a maid for someone like Simon Sheffield." If Derek noticed her discomfort it didn't stop him. "When I was ten or eleven my mother took me to work with her one day—I can't recall why. It was as unreal as going to the moon. There was a big swimming pool and a tennis court in back of this grand, two-story Tudor house. I saw a way of life I couldn't even comprehend."

"As a child perhaps, but since you've grown up I'm sure you've been in homes like those. Especially in your business."

"Yes, but when I walk in I always feel ten years old again."

"I can't give you confidence, Derek," Sabrina said slowly. "That's something you have to develop for yourself."

115

"Just being with you gives me confidence. The fact that you enjoy my company enough to spend time with me. And you must have enjoyed yourself the other night or you wouldn't have agreed to see me again," he said eagerly.

Sabrina didn't honestly find Derek that stimulating. In addition, her conscience hurt at the way she was using him. It made her reply warmer than it normally would have been. She managed to keep him happy and still tell part of the truth. "I wouldn't be having nearly as good a time this evening if I weren't here."

Derek glowed under the imagined compliment. He reached over and covered her hand with his. "I hope this is the beginning of a long friendship, Sabrina."

The waiter appeared to take their order, saving her the necessity of a reply.

During dinner Derek seemed bent on compiling a complete dossier on Sabrina. Since his questions weren't really personal, she couldn't very well object. He didn't ask anything about Josh or her marriage; he seemed more interested in her early life with Simon. Realizing his rather pathetic interest in what he considered the privileged classes, she indulged him, although his questions bordered on the tasteless.

"I suppose you had a governess when you were growing up," he remarked.

"I was too old for a governess." Sabrina smiled. "I would have been insulted."

"I'll bet it's the only thing you didn't have."

"Grandfather was very good to me," she acknowledged. "He gave me everything I asked for. He still does, as a matter of fact." She looked down at her plate, missing the flare of unreadable emotion in Derek's eyes. Sabrina was reflecting on the thing Simon had given her that she *didn't* want. She continued after a momentary hesitation. "But

116

don't think I was a spoiled little rich girl. I had to toe a very strict line. You probably had a lot more freedom than I."

Derek shrugged. "It's different with a boy."

"Not if you'd been Simon's grandson. Life wouldn't have been all swimming pools and tennis courts. He's just as tough on the people he loves as the ones he employs."

"Your husband doesn't seem to have any trouble with him. He's your grandfather's right-hand man, isn't he?"

"Josh is a lot like Grandfather," Sabrina answered tersely, deciding the time had come to change the subject. "How did you happen to become an actor?"

Derek seemed to realize that he had overstepped some boundary. He accepted her lead without comment, smiling wryly. "It's one of the jobs where you don't need a college degree."

Sabrina frowned. "Was it what you really wanted to do?"

He shrugged. "It's a living."

"Didn't you ever have a special ambition when you were young?" she persisted.

"I wouldn't have minded being a doctor or a lawyer. Those fellows have it made in the shade—big fees and bankers' hours."

She raised a delicate eyebrow. "Perhaps it's just as well that you didn't go into those professions."

"I didn't mean that the way it sounded," he said hurriedly. "I really did want to be a lawyer. There must be something very satisfying about getting up in front of a jury and being able to convince them that your client is innocent. Maybe I became an actor as the next best thing."

"But you should never settle for second best," Sabrina said earnestly. "Why didn't you make a stab at it?"

"Do you know how long it takes to get through law school, not counting the four years of college first? In my

117

profession if I get one big break I can make more than those guys will after ten years."

So much for the noble desire to defend the downtrodden, Sabrina thought cynically. Why had she ever thought Derek was amusing? He certainly wasn't the answer to her problem.

Derek had depth of perception, however. He sensed her disapproval and hastened to try to deflect it. For the remainder of dinner he exerted himself to be entertaining, making her laugh with outrageous stories about the people he worked with. She started to enjoy herself instead of just pretending to.

Although Sabrina had intended to make it a short evening, she found herself agreeing when Derek suggested they have dessert and espresso. He was a very shallow man and his reasons for wanting to be with her were unworthy, yet she couldn't help feeling sorry for him. Derek was the kind of person who tried to take shortcuts all his life, not realizing they would never get him anywhere.

Still, he could be quite amusing, and it was better than sitting alone by a telephone that didn't ring. Sabrina realized that she was postponing the moment when she would have to go home to an empty bed in a silent house.

About eleven o'clock she told Derek she had to leave. He regretfully took her back to her car. "I wish I could take you home," he said. "Would you like me to follow you?"

"No, I'll be fine. Thanks, Derek, for a lovely time."

"We'll have to do it again soon."

She smiled at him, reaching to turn the key in the ignition. "Good night."

"Sabrina, wait!" He put both hands on the door, leaning down to look in at her. "I will see you again, won't I?"

She hesitated. "I don't know, Derek. It depends on a lot of things."

"Did I say anything tonight to annoy you? Did I ask too many questions?" He seemed genuinely upset.

"No, it was a fun evening," she answered gently. It had been actually, once she had established the boundaries.

"Then why don't you want to see me again?"

"I didn't say that. I just—"

"Honey, I know a brushoff when I hear one."

"It isn't that, honestly. It just depends on when Josh gets home, and . . . and when he leaves again."

"Can I call you?"

"No, don't do that! Not that I'm hiding anything from Josh," she explained carefully. "It's just that the servants might get the wrong idea."

"What if I call you at work? Maybe we can have lunch someday."

"That's possible. And now I really must go, Derek. I'll never get up in the morning."

Sabrina was pleasantly tired driving home. She had a feeling that she would sleep soundly that night—unlike the one before when she had lain rigid in bed, staring at the ceiling then tossing restlessly most of the night. Getting out of the house had helped to put things into a better perspective. None of the problems had vanished, but at least she no longer felt like the central figure in a Greek tragedy.

She decided to leave her car in the driveway instead of putting it away. When she entered the house and started down the hall, she saw the light coming from the bedroom. Sabrina's relaxed body suddenly stiffened. Could Josh have come home? It was more likely that Michiko had left the light on for her, she reminded herself. But when she entered the bedroom, Josh was indeed there.

He had taken off his coat and tie, and unbuttoned his shirt almost down to his navel, but other than that he was fully dressed. The tension in his long body was almost

119

palpable. He looked as though he had been pacing the floor —a leashed wolf ready to break its chain. They stared at each other for a nerve-quivering moment.

It could have been a replay of the first night she had been out with Derek, except that Josh's anger was more controlled this time. There was no doubt that he was in a rage, however, and this time Sabrina knew their confrontation would end differently.

"When did you get home?" she asked, taking the offensive.

"About three hours ago," he answered evenly.

She walked over to the closet, taking off her jacket and hanging it up. "It's quite late by New York time. I'm surprised you're not already asleep."

"It's quite late by California time too. Where have you been until this hour, Sabrina?" His voice was nonetheless deadly for being so quiet.

"I went out to dinner."

"Michiko told me that much. I want to know with whom."

She turned around to face him, lifting her chin. "A friend."

Josh's eyes were as hard as the topaz they resembled. "The name, please."

"You have no right to cross-examine me like a common criminal! There are some questions I could ask *you.*"

"I thought you were the one with all the answers," he observed sarcastically.

"That's what bothers you, isn't it?" she taunted.

"I see you've been nursing your theory all the time I've been gone," he remarked ironically.

She refused to be put on the defensive. "What else did I have to do?"

A muscle worked at the point of his square jaw. "It appears that you found something."

"And if I did, what concern is that of yours?"

Josh looked pointedly at his watch, his grim smile holding no humor. "I believe we've just broken our own record for getting into an argument."

"I didn't start it, you did."

"By asking where you've been? I think that's a fair question for a husband to ask his wife when she comes drifting in at almost midnight."

"When did you develop this burning interest?" Sabrina's bitterness showed. "Certainly not in New York, since you didn't bother to phone."

Some of the anger left Josh's face. He turned away, jamming his hands in his pockets. "I didn't think you wanted to hear from me."

"That's as good an excuse as any."

The hard gleam was back in his eyes. "You didn't exactly send me off with a hug and a kiss."

"I didn't *send* you anyplace. You went—without telling me when you'd be back."

"I see," he drawled. "That's what this is all about. I wasn't supposed to know about your outside activities."

"I don't notice you telling me about yours," she muttered.

"There weren't any," he answered crisply. "I went to New York on business."

"A classic excuse. One you've used before," she added significantly.

Josh made a disgusted sound deep in his throat. "If that's another reference to that night with Pam, I offered to explain but you said you didn't want to hear it. As far as I'm concerned the subject is closed."

"How very convenient!"

He looked at her consideringly. "*Do* you want to hear about it?"

"No, she isn't really the problem." That wasn't so. The

121

thought of *any* other woman in Josh's arms hurt unbearably. But Sabrina wouldn't give him the satisfaction of knowing. It was a weapon he would use against her without hesitation.

"That's true. Our problems are more basic than that," he answered slowly. "I went to New York to give us both time to cool off. I thought it would be best if we didn't say a lot of things we'd regret later."

"Was that the reason, Josh? Or was I supposed to miss you so desperately that I'd throw myself in your arms when you came back, beg you to make love to me? Well, I'm sorry to disappoint you, but you aren't *that* good."

"Really, Sabrina?"

His eyes traveled slowly down from her throat, lingering on her pointed breasts, her hips, then the point where her slim thighs joined her body. Sabrina's cheeks flushed. If he had undressed her physically it couldn't have been more devastating. The blood raced wildly through her veins as her body responded to him without her volition.

"That wasn't the impression you've given me night after night," he continued mockingly. "I could make love to you right now, in spite of all your high indignation."

"Don't you dare touch me!" She gasped, clenching her fists until her nails bit cruelly into her palms. Sabrina knew her self-respect depended on resisting him.

"I have no intention of touching you. Your devious little mind would translate it into rape—after you'd enjoyed yourself thoroughly," he added derisively.

Sabrina was swept by burning anger. Josh knew perfectly well how he affected her. He could arouse her with a few murmured words, delight her with a touch. Her feeble attempt to taunt him had backfired, but it wasn't the only arrow in her quiver!

She forced herself to answer calmly. "I wouldn't count on sex to maintain your male supremacy. You aren't the

122

only man eager to please me." Sabrina had the satisfaction of seeing her barb strike home.

Josh's face darkened dangerously. Grasping her upper arm, he jerked her toward him. "If I didn't know you were trying to get a rise out of me—"

She looked up at him triumphantly. "Are you absolutely sure, Josh?"

His eyes were a narrow gleam of molten amber. "We've been a long time getting around to it, but now I want to know exactly where you were tonight—and with whom."

This time she didn't try to evade the question. "I went out to dinner with Derek Devlin."

For a moment Josh looked blank. "Who?"

"Derek Devlin, the man I met at the premiere."

"That two-bit actor?" he asked incredulously.

"I didn't know you were such a snob," she observed disdainfully. "Derek might not know much about mergers and stock issues, but I consider that a pure plus. He's a very charming man. We had a lot of fun together." Sabrina could see Josh's fury mounting.

"Exactly how much fun did you have?"

"A lot." She stared back at him defiantly.

"Did you go to bed with him?" Josh was controlling himself with an effort.

Sabrina was sick inside at the way things had gotten out of hand, but she wouldn't back down. "I don't have to answer that."

He swore viciously. "Yes, you damn well do! You're my wife!"

A demon was driving her on and Sabrina was powerless to stop it. "That's only a formality now," she replied tautly.

"Listen to me, Sabrina, and listen well." Josh's fingers tightened painfully around her arm. "I agreed to your terms about living together platonically, but if you think

I'm going to stand by tamely while you sleep with other men, you're going to find out differently—to your sorrow. Now I'm going to ask you one more time. Did you go to bed with him?"

Sabrina wondered fleetingly what Josh would do if she said yes, but she decided not to find out. Lying had done their relationship no good in the past. "No," she muttered unwillingly.

His tense body relaxed. He released her, putting distance between them as though he didn't trust himself.

Sabrina couldn't help feeling relief, although she didn't think Josh was capable of hurting her physically. But now that he was no longer threatening, the injustice of the thing galled her. It was the old double standard all over again. He could do what he wanted but she couldn't!

"How would you like it if I made a big screaming scene when *you* came home?" she demanded.

"You have," he replied briefly.

It wasn't the same thing and Josh knew it! "I've put up with your inquisition tonight, but I don't expect to go through this again," she said coldly.

"Nor do I." His voice carried an implicit warning that strengthened Sabrina's determination.

"You don't own me, Josh, contrary to what you may think. If it's all right for you to lead your own life, then I deserve the same privilege."

"Up to a point." He looked at her speculatively. "But you're right, perhaps I did overreact. I know you, Sabrina. You're not going to engage in a cheap affair just to spite me."

She couldn't very well deny it, but Sabrina pointed out something else that was true. "Maybe not, but I've changed in other ways. I don't intend to sit home alone while you're out doing your thing."

"You're proposing an open marriage, I take it. You go

124

your way and I go mine. Do we compare notes when we meet?" he asked sardonically.

The hopelessness of the situation made Sabrina want to cry. What made her think they could go on like this? For Josh it was a mere inconvenience, for her it would be a slow death. She couldn't live in the same house with him, sleep in the same bed, and know it was all a mockery. No amount of scandal would be worse than that.

"It won't work, Josh," she said slowly, keeping her voice steady through a great effort. "I'm going to get a divorce."

His expression hardened. "I thought we settled all that a few nights ago."

She shook her head wearily. "I don't care anymore what people think. I just want my freedom."

"And if I won't give it to you?"

"You can't hold me against my will."

"Perhaps not, but I don't have to make it easy for you. There's another thing you should think of. Simon is going to be very upset about this."

"He's the one who got me into it!" she exclaimed indignantly.

"Because he's convinced that we love each other." Josh's smile was mirthless. "And *he* hasn't changed his opinion."

"I'm through letting Simon or anyone else manipulate me," she replied bitterly. "If he wants to believe in fairy tales with happy endings, that's his problem."

"He loves you very much, Sabrina," Josh said softly. "Simon told me himself that you're the most important thing in his life."

All the happy years rose up to plague Sabrina. The years when she was growing up and her grandfather changed his whole life-style to make her the center of his world.

"I love him too," she said uncertainly. "But I'm a grown

woman now. He has to realize that I'm old enough to make my own decisions."

"To Simon you'll always be his little girl—the only person in the world capable of hurting him."

The blatant attempt to influence her enraged Sabrina. Did Josh take her for a fool? "Simon Sheffield is one of the world's toughest people. He'll survive," she replied curtly.

"Are you so sure? Haven't you ever wondered what part our divorce played in his heart attack—because that wasn't faked, even if the relapse was."

Her face turned white. "That's a rotten guilt trip to try to lay on me!"

"I'm not blaming you, I'm just telling you to think out all the consequences of what you're contemplating. You weren't here so you didn't see the difference in him after you left. He was hurting a lot. Maybe he would have had the heart attack anyway, but now that he's had one, are you willing to take a chance that your actions won't provoke another?"

Sabrina was torn in different directions. She realized what Josh was doing, yet there was a grain of truth in what he said. Hadn't she asked herself the same terrible questions when her invincible grandfather was stricken? She felt the jaws of a trap closing around her.

"I can't be expected to give up my whole life for a mere supposition," she said helplessly. "Maybe if we explained it to him together. We could say that it was an amicable thing, that we . . . that it just didn't work out. Surely then he wouldn't be as upset."

Josh shook his head. "Don't count on me to do your dirty work for you. I'm not the one who wants the divorce."

She looked at him in outrage. "You'd jeopardize Simon's health, the man who's been like a grandfather to you too?"

Josh was a modern Samson, pulling down the pillars. He

would destroy them all if he couldn't have his own way. But unlike Samson, Josh didn't have any vulnerable spots. What was it Derek had called him—a shark? That's what he was like, sleek and deadly, with no conscience and no mercy.

He shrugged. "What do I have to lose?"

He waited, staring at her with an enigmatic expression. Sabrina stared back at him, her eyes a blazing green in her pale face. As she ran shaking fingers through her long golden hair, something flickered in the depths of his tawny eyes.

"I can't believe you'd be so rotten," she whispered.

"I'll never let you go if I can help it, Sabrina." His voice was quiet, but it had the finality of bars clanging shut.

CHAPTER EIGHT

The next weeks were the most miserable of Sabrina's life, although their strained relationship didn't seem to affect Josh. Having settled everything to his own satisfaction, his behavior was completely normal. In fact, it was too normal to suit Sabrina.

Taking up their everyday life meant accepting invitations from friends. Sabrina was reluctant, fearing that their estrangement would show, but no one would have guessed from Josh's conduct. He was totally relaxed in company, putting his arm around Sabrina and teasing her the way he used to do.

In the beginning she had stiffened resentfully, suspecting that he was taunting her. But there were no sly little innuendoes in his banter, no liberties taken in his casual affection. Josh had merely slipped back into their old ways.

At first Sabrina resented it, then she unconsciously started to emulate him. It was so easy to slide her arm around his waist as they stood chatting in a group. It was a contact that was denied to her anywhere else. She had to resist the urge to trace the line of his lean rib cage with her fingers or rub her cheek against his solid shoulder. Those actions weren't necessary to keep up the farce of their happy marriage. If she gave in to the overwhelming urge, Josh would know how much she hungered for him.

Her own knowledge of that fact was humiliating

enough. It was even more shattering when she had to admit to herself that what she felt was a great deal more than basic passion. She was still in love with Josh. In spite of his deviousness, his blinding ambition, his infidelity, she still loved him with all her heart.

Expressed that bluntly it sounded insane, but his good qualities were equally impressive. They had nothing to do with the searing physical attraction between them. Josh was witty and intelligent; he was the best companion she'd ever had. In the good days they had enjoyed each other's company, not needing anyone else. He was kind and dependable in a crisis—the strength he had given her during Simon's illness had been all that had gotten her through—and he was generous to a fault.

It wasn't long after the traumatic night of their showdown that Josh came home with a small, gaily wrapped box. It was accompanied by a long white envelope.

"What's this?" she asked warily.

"Why don't you open it and see?" He smiled.

Inside was a gold pin in the shape of a star. "What's this for?" she asked.

"The card will explain."

It was a humorous card of congratulations, showing a tired, happy mountaineer sprawling across Mount Everest. "I don't understand," she murmured.

"Remember when you were little and you got a gold star for every A on your report card? Well, this is a belated one." Josh's voice was husky. "I always felt badly that your raise came on the day we had our argument."

Sabrina's first impulse was to throw her arms around his neck. Her next reaction was suspicion. It was a very clever gesture that was calculated to lower her defenses. "It was no big deal, you didn't have to do this," she said negligently.

The tender look on Josh's face faded. "Forget it." He shrugged. "I would have done as much for any friend."

"But we aren't—" She stopped abruptly.

"Friends?" he finished for her, his mouth twisting in a mocking smile. "No—we're married." He turned and walked out of the room, leaving her clutching the small box.

Sabrina was able to parry Josh's thrusts during the day, but the nights tried her mettle. He insisted on being as casual in the bedroom as he was everywhere else. Although Sabrina had long since taken to wearing nightgowns, Josh continued to sleep in the nude. She had learned to keep her eyes glued to a book while he undressed, but she was fully aware of him.

If he knew it, he gave no sign. Josh wandered around quite unostentatiously, not displaying himself, merely acting the way he always had. Every night tried Sabrina's resolve to the breaking point. She would *not* let her body betray her. It would be too degrading. Especially since Josh would misunderstand.

And then came the terrible night when she awoke in his arms. Sabrina had been having a recurrent dream where she was weaving her fingers through Josh's thick hair, murmuring his name as she molded her body to his. In her dream he had always caressed her tenderly, twining his legs around hers while he cupped her bottom to fit more closely to his pulsing loins. She would move against him in quivering anticipation, prolonging the exquisite sensations as long as she could.

But this night something was missing. Although his body was igniting hers like a bonfire, Josh wasn't responding. His lips were eluding hers. That wonderful, firm mouth wasn't exploring hers with passion, his tongue wasn't teasing with promises guaranteed to leave her throbbing.

130

Sabrina made a tiny sound in her sleep, pulling Josh's head down. For just a moment she experienced the rapture she was seeking. His warm mouth closed over hers with a desperate hunger as his arms closed tightly around her. He rolled her onto her back, crushing her slender body into the mattress with his strength. But when she clasped her arms around his neck and arched her hips into his, Josh groaned deeply, putting his hands on her shoulders to lever himself away.

It was the groan that woke her. Sabrina opened her eyes to find Josh's head poised over hers. There was no way she could accuse him of being the aggressor. Her arms were still around his neck and he was resisting the pressure she was putting on them. She came awake instantly—awake and terribly embarrassed.

She removed her arms hurriedly, scooting back to her own side of the bed. "I—I'm sorry," she muttered, thankful that the darkness hid her burning cheeks.

"No harm done," he remarked, although his breathing sounded quickened.

"I was asleep," she explained carefully.

"I know."

His quiet answers didn't satisfy her. She felt a compulsion to make sure he understood. "It won't happen again."

"I certainly hope not." When she turned her head quickly, trying to gauge his expression in the darkness, Josh chuckled ruefully. "I'm not made of steel."

She digested that slowly. After a long moment she remarked tentatively, "I wouldn't have been able to stop you."

She could feel the movement as he shook his head. "No, my dear. I'm sure you know that I want you, but not if you aren't fully aware of what you're doing." There was quiet for a time, then he reached over and stroked her thigh. The sensuous feeling sent licking flames of excitement through

131

her. "You're awake now." The simple statement ended on a questioning note.

Sabrina tensed even further. Her aching, unfulfilled body begged her to give one answer, but her pride and common sense dictated another. If she gave in to Josh now, she would never be able to refuse him again.

Turning on the side away from him she said, "Good night, Josh."

A dinner at Simon's house proved to be the unwitting catalyst that upset their fragile truce. Her grandfather had been asking them for days, but Sabrina had managed to be evasive. Finally Simon forced her hand.

"You're still angry with me, aren't you?" he asked. He had called her at the office with yet another invitation that was really more of a command this time.

"You can hardly expect me to be overjoyed at being treated like a three-year-old," she remarked crisply, neither affirming nor denying his statement.

"When you act like one, you have to be treated like one."

Sabrina tried to control her annoyance. Simon would never change. "If you're looking for thanks, give to the Salvation Army," she advised him. "You can also use that as a tax deduction."

His imperious tone gave way to one of self-pity. "I know I'm just a foolish old man, but I was only doing what I thought you wanted."

"You have a mind like a computer and you hate to be thwarted," she remarked dryly. "You did what *you* wanted."

Simon dropped his playacting abruptly. "Okay, so I didn't have any right to meddle. But aren't you glad that I did?"

Sabrina couldn't force herself to answer. If Simon had

stayed out of it she would be in New York right now, resigned to the fact that she would never see Josh again. Maybe she would never have forgotten him, but at least there wouldn't be all these new memories to surmount— some of them terrible, but some so achingly sweet that they twisted her heart.

"Sabrina?" he asked sharply when the silence stretched out. "Is anything wrong?"

"No, I—I'm busy, Grandfather. I really have to go."

"You can spare me another minute," he said decisively. "Are you and Josh having problems?"

"How could we possibly? You wouldn't permit it." Her attempt at lightheartedness didn't come off.

"What's the matter this time?" Simon asked quietly.

"Nothing," she insisted quickly. "You're imagining things."

"I know you better than you know yourself, child. Is that why you won't come to dinner? Because you and Josh aren't speaking?"

"That's ridiculous!"

"Then how about tonight?"

"Well, I—I don't know if Josh has plans."

"I'll ask him," Simon stated, hanging up abruptly.

Sabrina realized that he only had to buzz Josh on the intercom. He would reach him long before she could get through the switchboard and several secretaries. Sabrina was fatalistic when Josh called her a short time later and they agreed this was one invitation they had very little choice about accepting.

As luck would have it, she was late getting home and had to rush to get ready. Sabrina was so wound up that she was like a primed rocket, ready to spin into orbit. Her hands were shaking so as she tried to put on makeup that things kept clattering onto the dressing table.

133

Josh put his hands on her shoulders. "Relax, Sabrina, you're as taut as a violin string."

Sabrina's eyes were jade green with emotion. "This isn't like going out with our friends, Josh."

"Sure it is." His long fingers kneaded her tense muscles in a soothing rhythm.

"No, Simon suspects something."

He stopped for a second before resuming his massage. "What makes you think so?" After Sabrina related their conversation, Josh was reassuring. "It doesn't sound too damaging to me."

"When I was little, Grandfather could always tell when I was lying," she said doubtfully.

Josh's hands moved around her neck to cup her chin. He tilted her head back, smiling down at her. "Then we'll just have to convince him, won't we?"

The lovely house she'd grown up in was as familiar to her as her current home, relaxing Sabrina slightly. She was aware of Simon's all-seeing gaze but there was nothing suspect in his greeting. They went into the billiard room to have a drink before dinner.

Josh suggested a game, which put Sabrina even more at ease. Simon was fiercely competitive. He wouldn't have time to give them assessing glances when all his attention was focused on winning. Was that what Josh had in mind? Had he done it for her sake? As she gazed at her husband consideringly, Josh's wink gave Sabrina the answer.

What a complex man he was, kind one moment and ruthless the next. Sabrina sipped her drink slowly, trying to figure him out. Of course it was to Josh's advantage also to keep her grandfather in the dark. Was that why he was working so hard at it? Before she could come to any conclusion, Simon demanded her attention.

"Come, my dear, let's go in to dinner," he said.

She gathered her thoughts with an effort. "Are you through with your game already?"

Josh's broad grin showed his even white teeth. "Your grandfather is losing. Does that give you a clue?"

"Nonsense! I can beat you any day of the week and twice on Sunday," the older man snapped. "I put myself through college hustling pigeons like you."

"Your father endowed the science wing, and you lived at the fraternity house," Josh replied calmly.

Simon chuckled. "Well, I *could* have put myself through. Besides, we're neglecting Sabrina. Have I told you that you're looking very lovely tonight, my dear?"

Sabrina smiled at the white-haired man who was such an integral part of her life. She really loved him very much in spite of everything. "You're looking quite fit too, Grandfather. No one would believe you were ever sick a day in your life."

It was said in all innocence, but Simon gazed at her sharply. "You know better than that, Sabrina," he said quietly. "You and Josh were what pulled me through."

A glance at his wife's troubled face told Josh some intervention was called for. "Then the least you could do is let me win at billiards," he remarked jokingly.

Simon wasn't willing to let the moment pass. He continued to stare at Sabrina, addressing his words to her. "It would kill me to think I made you unhappy for even one single minute."

She knew it was the kind of figure of speech that people used without meaning it literally, but her heart lurched in her breast. She tried to give him the reassurance he was seeking.

"What would I have to be unhappy about?" She managed a bright smile.

When he continued to search her expression, not completely satisfied with her answer, Josh took Sabrina's hands and drew her to her feet. "I think your grandfather is becoming a voyeur in his old age, but if that's what he wants I guess we'll have to give it to him. Shall we show him how much we love each other?"

Before she could stop him, he put his arms around her, urging her close. Sabrina's hands went defensively to his shoulders, her body stiffening to avoid contact with his. Josh's eyes were unfathomable as he bent his dark head, touching his mouth to hers.

Sabrina forced herself to relax, reminding herself why they were doing this. Josh was only trying to be convincing. So when his lips moved sensuously over hers and his hands wandered caressingly over her back, her lips parted and her arms clasped around Josh's neck. She was enveloped by him, every tactile sense responding to this man she loved so overwhelmingly. They were so lost in the wonder of each other that for a moment Simon's laughing comment didn't penetrate.

"Okay, children, remember this is just a rehearsal. You'd better save the real performance for a private showing."

Josh kept his arms around Sabrina as they drew apart slowly. She felt weightless in his embrace, as if she would rise to the ceiling if he didn't anchor her. When her confused eyes lifted to his, Josh leaned down and kissed her tenderly.

His voice was husky as he turned to Simon. "I suppose you'd have a fit if we left now?"

"Count on it!" Once his doubts were removed Simon was bubbling with good spirits. "A little self-control builds character."

"That's the sort of advice you're fond of giving, not taking," Josh joked.

Their good-natured banter went over Sabrina's head. She was worried about her free response to Josh's embrace.

136

Had she given herself away? Could Josh tell when it ceased to be for Simon's sake and became a compulsion of her own? But he was pretty ardent himself. It wasn't difficult for either of them since there had never been any question of their physical attraction. Maybe Josh would just chalk her response up to that, Sabrina consoled herself.

"Besides, we haven't had dinner yet," Simon was saying. "Maria promised me she was going to have something brown." Maria had been his cook for twenty years.

Sabrina realized his comment was directed at her. She looked puzzled, thinking she had missed part of the conversation. "Something brown?"

Josh laughed. "Haven't you ever heard your grandfather's theory? Only brown things are good to eat."

"Exactly." Simon nodded his head. "Steak, french fries, chocolate—they're all brown."

"Conversely, you never eat anything that's green," Josh explained. "That includes such unappealing items as broccoli, spinach, and lime gumdrops."

"If I didn't know you were kidding I'd report you to your doctor." Sabrina smiled.

"Doctors, what do they know?" Simon commented disparagingly.

The evening she had dreaded turned out to be enjoyable. They had shared so many dinners like this in the past. Conversation flowed easily and Sabrina savored the feeling of old times. She and Josh even exchanged private glances over some of Simon's more outrageous opinions. If the realization surfaced that their rapport would end with the evening, she refused to think of it.

Just when it appeared that dinner would be an unqualified success, Simon destroyed the possibility. It started out innocently enough with a mild difference of opinion with Josh that sounded more serious than it was. Simon pursued every idea with passion.

"I don't know why you don't agree with me on that restaurant chain." He frowned at Josh. "I think it would be a valuable acquisition."

"I've told you my objections," Josh answered evenly. "Our strength is in heavy industry. When you deal with the public directly, it's an entirely different operation—and not necessarily that lucrative. We have an obligation to the stockholders to make money."

Simon scowled. "That's right, go ahead and needle me."

Josh suppressed a smile with difficulty. "That wasn't my intention. When did you develop such a thin skin?"

"If there's one thing I can't stand it's a smug subordinate," Simon grumbled.

"What's going on?" Sabrina asked.

"Your grandfather is suffering from slightly faulty judgment," Josh told her. "His flyer into show business wasn't an unqualified success."

"You haven't won yet!" The older man's eyes glittered fiercely. "We haven't even explored television rights for the movie yet."

"You'd have to give away free cranberry sauce to get anyone to buy that turkey," Josh snorted.

"It wasn't that bad," Sabrina protested. "Some of the performances were quite good."

Josh's laughter died. "I don't think you're an unbiased critic," he remarked coldly.

"Why not? Because she's on my side? Sabrina is an average, ordinary movie-goer," Simon stated. It didn't bother him a bit that none of those descriptions fit her. "And she loved the movie."

From the austere look on Josh's face Sabrina knew that he thought she had given the film good marks on account of Derek. Actually his performance was one of the weak spots, but she wasn't going to tell Josh that.

"I didn't say I loved it," she explained carefully. "I just don't think it was the disaster that Josh does."

"Is that supposed to make me feel better?" Simon exploded indignantly. "He thinks it will lose a lot of money, and you think it will lose just a little. That's like being offered a choice between quitting and getting fired!"

"I'm sure it's not that big a deal to Ameropol," Sabrina remarked impatiently, annoyed that it should have come up at all to spoil things.

"You're right, we'll take a tax loss." Simon turned triumphantly to Josh. "If I manage to pull this thing into the black after all, you'll be singing another tune."

"It still won't be *Play It Again, Sam,*" Josh answered dryly.

"You don't think I have a future as a producer? Well, maybe you're right." Simon's blue eyes glinted with amusement as he switched gears. "It's going to hurt me to send back that casting couch I ordered, though."

The two men smiled at each other, good humor completely restored. "Has anyone ever told you that you're a dirty old man?" Josh asked.

"They wouldn't dare," Simon answered calmly.

Josh laughed. "That's true. The world wipes its nose when Simon Sheffield sneezes."

Simon's mirth deserted him. "That reminds me of the cold product Pam's division is having trouble with. I've been wanting to talk to you about it."

Josh's glance flicked to Sabrina for just an instant. "I think everything is under control there. As a matter of fact, it was an idea of Sabrina's that led us out of the woods." Josh explained about her suggestion.

"Very good, Sabrina." Simon's approval was brief. He turned back to Josh almost immediately. "There's one segment of the country that hasn't responded to our advertising campaign. It's the section where the lawsuit was filed, understandably enough. I want you to get together with Pam and see what you can do about it. The percentages can make a difference on her profit and loss sheet."

"I'll have to turn it over to Rollings," Josh answered. "The merger I'm putting together with Acme Steel and Amalgamated is taking up every minute of my day."

Simon's voice held irritation. "What's the matter with nights? Pam would be willing to work."

"Well, I wouldn't," Josh said decisively.

"Since when have you become a clock watcher?" the older man asked.

"I happen to have a life outside of Ameropol," Josh grated.

"Oh, for—!" Simon's annoyance was vocal. "Sabrina isn't a new bride! Besides that, she's a corporate wife. She understands these things."

"Does she?" Josh smiled sardonically.

"Of course she does! Don't you, Sabrina? You wouldn't mind if Josh had to work a couple of nights?"

"It's entirely up to him," she answered evenly.

Their eyes met and dueled. Josh's cynicism deepened as she said, "You've given me the same choice that Simon mentioned earlier."

"I don't know what's the matter with you!" Simon exclaimed. "You're acting as if there were something going on between you and Pam."

"I just don't want Sabrina to think there is," Josh explained carefully.

"How could she possibly?" Simon made no attempt to curb his irritation. "Pam is the head of one of our companies. She needs your help and I expect you to give it."

He refused to discuss it any further in spite of Josh's attempts. The matter was settled to Simon's satisfaction, and he refused to recognize the lack of enthusiasm that greeted his edict.

Sabrina and Josh left soon after dinner. They kept up appearances until they were in the car, then both were silent.

"You're very quiet, Sabrina," Josh observed finally. "Are you tired?"

"A little."

"But that isn't the reason, is it?" Characteristically, Josh went right to the point. "You're thinking about Pam, aren't you?"

She didn't try to evade either. "I believe it's natural under the circumstances."

"This was all Simon's idea. I had nothing to do with it."

"Except to say that you couldn't find time to see her during the day."

Josh's strong hands gripped the wheel until his knuckles turned white. "I'm handling a merger between two multi-million-dollar companies. It has a definite bearing on how our stock behaves in the coming months. And I was *trying* to get out of seeing her at all, trying to avoid the very suspicions I'm getting from you now."

She turned to look out the window. "You don't have to convince me."

"I don't think I could," he answered somberly. "You've made up your mind that Pam and I are going to use this as an excuse to make mad, passionate love. Isn't that true?"

"What you do doesn't really concern me any longer."

"Are you giving me your blessing?" he asked sardonically.

She stared out into the darkness, seeing images that made her shrivel inside. Josh making love to Pam, caressing her as only he knew how to do, laughing softly with her at little private jokes. Sabrina drew in her breath, willing the odious pictures out of her mind.

"You never needed my permission before," she said bitterly. "Why are you asking for it now?"

141

Josh hesitated a moment. When he spoke his voice was husky. "Tonight at Simon's, for a little while things were the way they used to be between us."

"We're both superb actors," she observed coldly.

"No, Sabrina. When I kissed you that wasn't acting—on either of our parts. I know every reaction of your lovely body. I felt you tremble in my arms, felt the total response you couldn't hide. Can't we go back and start all over?"

It was too much to expect that Josh had been fooled. Added to her frustration was burning anger. "You don't give up. You want it all, don't you? Ameropol, me, *and* Pam. At least I *hope* I get middle billing."

Josh pulled into their driveway and switched off the motor. He turned her to him. "You're the only one I want. How can I get that through your head? Let me love you," he pleaded, trying to draw her closer.

It was a temptation she didn't dare consider. Nothing had really changed; Josh was just playing on her weakness. "You'll have to settle for two out of three," she said crisply.

Josh's temper suddenly ignited. His eyes were blazing, and yet cold at the same time. "All right, have it your own way, Sabrina. I'm through trying to reach you on any level. I've explained, I've apologized, I've done everything except crawl. If that's what you're waiting for, forget it! From now on we'll each lead our own lives. Is that what you want?"

"I—I think it's for the best." What else could she say?

"Good, you've got it!" He opened the car door and got out, slamming it viciously behind him.

Sabrina remained in her seat, watching his long body stride toward the house. Her heart was so heavy that it was an actual pain in her breast. How could the evening have ended like this after such a bright beginning?

Josh opened the door, looking back over his shoulder. "Come on," he ordered curtly.

"I'll be there in a minute." She needed a little time alone.

"You'll come in now," he ordered.

Sabrina's misery coalesced into one burning lump of resentment. "Is that what you call going our separate ways? You do what you want and *I* do what you want!"

He strode back to the car. "You don't have to be in love with someone to care about their safety. I'm not going to leave you out here alone."

He didn't have to put his feelings into such bald words. Sabrina searched for something that would hurt him as much as he was hurting her. "I'd forgotten what a valuable possession I am," she said caustically. "You have to be sure the golden goose is safely put away, don't you?"

He jerked open the door and pulled her out of the car, toward the front door. As soon as they were inside he dropped her arm and headed for the bedroom. Sabrina followed more slowly, trying to master her temper. She wanted to yell and scream at him, to pound his chest with her fists. But something warned her that this wasn't the time.

Josh was flinging off his clothes in a controlled rage; the air fairly crackled with it. Sabrina took her nightgown and went into the bathroom in a resentful silence. When she came out he was in bed lying on his back with one arm over his eyes. She got into bed and turned off the lights without saying good night.

They both lay there pretending to sleep, each knowing the other was awake. The tension could almost be felt. Could they go on like this night after night? Or was that what Josh was counting on—that she would crack first? Sabrina's small chin set stubbornly. She could take it as long as he could.

Very deliberately she turned on her side.

CHAPTER NINE

The weeks that followed were like a nightmare. If Sabrina had thought their former estrangement was difficult, this was a thousand times worse. After the evening at Simon's house, with its traumatic ending, Josh was icily polite to her.

The next morning he had informed Michiko that he wouldn't be home for dinner. Sabrina had made no comment, although she was seething inside with hurt, anger, and disappointment. It was too much to expect that their relations would be anything approaching normal for a while, yet Sabrina had secretly hoped that Josh would reconsider about working nights with Pam. It would show that he was as miserable as she over the present situation and wanted to remedy it. But he was sending her a clear signal; Josh was accepting her terms.

It was no hardship for him to go his own way unencumbered, Sabrina reflected bitterly. But if he expected her to wait around for him patiently, he was badly mistaken. Fortunately she had friends of her own.

Sabrina called Derek as soon as she got to the office. "Did I wake you?" she asked when his unmistakably sleepy voice answered. "I'm sorry, but I didn't even expect you to be there. I was going to leave a message with your answering service."

"I'm not working today. As a matter of fact I'm between

assignments." He laughed. "Which is Hollywood talk for being unemployed."

"That's too bad."

"It's only temporary. My agent is discussing a couple of deals." He shrugged the matter off as unimportant, his voice warming. "It's wonderful to hear from you, Sabrina. I called your office a couple of times but you were always in a meeting or out someplace."

She had gotten his messages and ignored them. Sabrina felt a white lie was in order. "I'm afraid things are sometimes disorganized around here."

"No problem, I'm just glad we finally got together. I hope you're calling to say you can meet me for lunch."

"Well, actually, I was thinking of dinner. If you're not busy tonight, that is."

"Never too busy for you." His voice was jubilant. It turned casual as he said, "Is your husband on the road again?"

She matched her tone to his. "No, Josh is in town but he has to work the next few nights and I get terribly bored just waiting for him to come home."

"That's understandable." From the abstraction in his voice it was evident that Derek was trying to appraise the situation.

Sabrina was not without conscience. She couldn't use him shamelessly. "The rules are still the same, Derek, so if you want to refuse, please feel free. My feelings won't be hurt."

"Why would I do that? I'm delighted. Shall we try the Wedgwood Room tonight? Would you like to meet me at the same time?"

"That would be fine. Or you can pick me up at home," she added deliberately. After all, she had nothing to hide.

Derek hesitated for a moment as he swam in unfamiliar waters. "That sounds even better," he agreed tentatively.

Sabrina smiled ruefully as she hung up. Poor Derek, he was thoroughly confused. She would have to be very careful tonight not to give him any inkling that her marriage was in trouble. Besides the obvious reason, it would shatter his image of money being the panacea for all ills.

Derek's demonstrated pleasure in her company that evening was balm to Sabrina's wounded spirit. He was as properly respectful as always, but his admiring glances told her that he would be happy to see their friendship deepen. It was what she needed at this low point in her life, but she was careful not to hold out any hope.

Derek was extremely perceptive where she was concerned, following her lead carefully. He didn't refer to his disadvantaged youth again, and he kept his compliments within the boundaries of simple courtesy. The only sticky point in the evening occurred when he brought up the subject of his recent movie.

"What did your grandfather have to say about it?" he asked eagerly.

Sabrina thought back to the evening at Simon's house when he had tried to defend his judgment. The investment had been insignificant to Ameropol. It wasn't the loss that bothered Simon, it was being proven wrong in a difference of opinion with Josh. She couldn't tell Derek that, however. It was a matter of burning importance to him.

"Oh, he—he told Josh that he expected it to show a profit." That wasn't really a lie. A tax loss was an advantage of sorts.

"Really?" Derek's eyes gleamed with excitement. "I thought he might have been put off because the reviews weren't exactly great."

Sabrina smiled wryly. "Grandfather doesn't pay any attention to other people's opinions—especially when they differ from his."

"That's fantastic! Do you think he might make more movies?"

Her lips curved in amusement. "It wouldn't surprise me, if only to prove something to Josh."

"Your husband doesn't approve?"

"Josh's approval varies with the prevailing climate," she answered bitterly, regretting it immediately. "Could you catch the waiter's eye? I'd like some more coffee," she said, aware of Derek's discreetly assessing glance.

When he took her home Sabrina was braced for the inevitable confrontation with Josh. She was cloaked in righteous indignation and ready with all her arguments, but Josh wasn't home. After the bright flame of her anger burned down, Sabrina was desolate. He couldn't be conducting business until this hour, and he didn't care that she knew it. Josh wasn't even bothering to pretend.

She was just hanging up her dress when he came in, looking completely drained. There were deep lines in his face, but his dark suit and white linen shirt were as immaculate as always. Why not? Sabrina thought bitterly. He must have folded them carefully. The knowledge made her stiff with fury.

"I thought you'd be asleep," Josh remarked, momentary surprise penetrating his weariness.

"I just got home," she answered coolly.

His long fingers paused in the act of unknotting his tie. "I should have known."

As his eyes slid over her, Sabrina realized that she was standing there in just her bra and pantyhose. She slipped quickly into a yellow satin robe. "There wasn't any reason for me to stay home."

"I suppose not," he replied indifferently. He went into the bathroom.

Sabrina had put on her nightgown and gotten into bed by the time he came out. She didn't pretend to be asleep,

148

however. "I assume your evening was satisfactory," she commented.

"About what I expected." He started to get undressed.

This time Sabrina didn't avert her eyes. If Josh could pretend that it was normal under the circumstances, she could too. Let's see just how unself-conscious he was.

As if aware of her scrutiny, Josh looked up. "Checking for evidence, Sabrina?"

Her cheeks bloomed with color but she forced herself to be as derisive as he. "That's not the way one discovers it, but I'm not interested enough to prove the point."

He grinned briefly. "It's a good thing, because I'm too tired to put up a strong defense."

Sabrina breathed a little more freely when he got under the covers. It allowed her to give full attention to her grievance. "You're lucky we've come to an agreement. It would be difficult for you to play two roles."

He adjusted the pillow under his head to a more comfortable angle. "Isn't that what you think I've been doing?"

"You didn't exactly protest too vigorously when the opportunity was presented to you," she said bitterly.

"How about you, Sabrina?" Josh levered himself up on an elbow to look down at her.

"What did you expect me to do, tell Grandfather I wouldn't permit you to work nights? That would have gone over big!"

"I'm not talking about that. Isn't all of this fuss and fury because *you* want to do *your* own thing?"

"How can you even think that?" She gasped.

"Perhaps I learned from you." In the filtered light from the window his face was hard.

"Josh, you can't—"

"I'm tired, Sabrina. I'm going to sleep."

Josh shifted onto his stomach with his face turned away

from her. In just a few minutes his even breathing told that he was asleep. It was a surcease that was denied to Sabrina.

That night set the pattern for the following ones. Josh worked late the rest of the week, and Sabrina saw Derek on many of the nights. She and Josh didn't argue again, but they were growing farther and farther apart. The weekend brought things to a head.

They had a date on Saturday night to go to the theater with two old friends, Trina and Dudley Creighton. After the play, which was a light comedy, they went out for a late supper.

As they sat in the restaurant discussing the performance, Dudley observed, "It was very amusing but not very believable. If she suspected her husband of chasing around, why didn't she just confront him with it instead of plotting that elaborate revenge? Then she would have found out the poor soul was only planning a surprise party for their anniversary."

"And there wouldn't have been any story," his wife pointed out.

"That's true," he admitted.

"Besides, how do you calmly look at your husband and remark, 'I understand you're having an affair with our next-door neighbor.'"

"Trina's right." Josh's face was coolly amused. "It's something a man would do but never a woman. She would decide to get even by going out with other men—the kind she'd never look at ordinarily."

Josh's veiled remark wasn't lost on Sabrina. She masked her anger and replied in the same light tone. "Maybe it would turn out to be a good thing. She might find out what she's been missing."

Dudley looked puzzled. "Why would it be a good thing if their marriage broke up over a misunderstanding?"

150

To the others it appeared that Josh was smiling fondly at his wife. They didn't notice the sardonic twist to his mouth. "Sabrina doesn't always bother about end results when she gets carried away."

"You're right, darling." The smile she gave him was equally false. "I'm not nearly as good as you when it comes to plotting."

The conversation turned to other things, but Sabrina's anger simmered under the surface. She waited until they were at home to challenge Josh over his unfair tactics.

"I suppose those little barbed remarks amused you tonight," she flared, flinging her coat on the bed.

"Yours or mine?" he asked, unperturbed.

"I was only defending myself against all of your double-edged remarks!"

Josh paused to look at her from head to toe. "The term iron butterfly was invented for you, my dear. You're about as defenseless as a man-eating tiger."

Is that what he really thought? Didn't he know these arguments were killing her a little bit at a time? They stared at each other, both as taut as karate experts anticipating the next move. Josh didn't see that it was unshed tears that were turning her green eyes so bright.

An expression of terrible weariness settled over his face, making him look suddenly older. "You evidently thrive on these little set-tos, Sabrina, but they're beginning to pall on me. From now on I'm going to sleep in the guest room."

She went deathly pale, her eyes the only spot of color in her white face. It was yet another tear in the rapidly shredding fabric of their marriage. When they shared a bedroom, no matter how difficult it was at times, they were together at least physically.

"But you said that we should . . ." Her stumbling words came to a halt.

"Keep up appearances for the servants?" he finished

151

mockingly. "After what's been going on around here, I think they've formed a few conclusions."

The whole atmosphere of the house changed after that. It was as though something ominous was about to happen —except that Sabrina knew it already had. The Japanese couple was inevitably affected. Their former broad smiles were almost never in evidence. It was a relief to leave the house every morning and a chore to return to it.

Josh was no longer working nights, but it wasn't much of an improvement. On the evenings that he and Sabrina dined at home, they made courteous conversation during dinner. Trying to avoid all the trouble spots didn't leave much to talk about. After dinner Josh worked on papers that he brought home, while Sabrina read or did work of her own. At the end of the evening they would go to their respective rooms.

Sabrina hadn't seen Derek in over a week. He called her often at work, but she just didn't feel up to socializing.

One morning Derek called when Sabrina was feeling especially low. "I'm going to make you an offer you can't refuse," he announced. "How would you like to meet Sir Frank Manning at a cast party on the set of *Eagles at Dawn?*"

Manning was a famous actor who was making a much-talked-about movie in America. The charismatic Englishman was noted for his bursts of temperament that occasionally closed the set. "How did you manage to wangle an invitation?" Sabrina asked.

Derek answered smugly, "You're not the only one with connections. How about it? I'll pick you up around seven thirty."

"Well, I—" She hesitated. Sabrina knew she should refuse, but it was a great temptation. She hadn't done anything that was fun in a long time.

"I haven't seen you in days and this is something special," Derek wheedled. "I'd ask your husband to join us except that it's strictly by invitation and I can bring only one guest. Couldn't you explain it to him?"

That was the deciding factor. Why should she have to explain anything to Josh when he didn't extend her the same courtesy? If he had somewhere to go he just went!

After she hung up Sabrina called Michiko to tell her she wouldn't be home for dinner. "Did . . . uh . . . is Mr. Winchester going to be out?"

"He didn't mention it." The housekeeper's voice was neutral.

Sabrina had secretly hoped that Josh might be going out too, but it didn't matter, she assured herself. Still, she managed to find last-minute things to do in the office. When she returned home there was only time to dash in and freshen up.

Josh greeted her with surprise. "Michiko said you were going out."

"I am. I just came home to change clothes." Sabrina beat a hasty retreat into the bedroom.

She had expected to be at the front door when Derek arrived, but a torn pair of hose delayed her. When she hurried down the hall there were voices in the entry. Josh and Derek were standing together in the foyer.

Sabrina was immediately struck by the difference in the two men. Josh had changed to jeans and a navy polo shirt. Derek had on an expensive sport coat and perfectly pressed gray slacks, but Josh was the more quietly elegant of the two. There was an innate air of assurance about him that reduced Derek to the status of a door-to-door salesman.

Derek had recognized the gap between them without ever meeting Josh. He was looking extremely ill at ease now that they were face to face, although Josh's manners couldn't be faulted. They were correct if not warm. Sabrina called up all of her own poise as she joined them.

When they were in the car a few minutes later, Derek looked uncomfortable. "I didn't know your husband was going to be home. I wouldn't . . . that is . . . you could have met me somewhere if it was more convenient."

"It wasn't."

He stared at her grim profile out of the corner of his eye. "I wouldn't want your husband to get the wrong idea."

"I doubt that he's given it any thought." Sabrina couldn't help the bitterness that crept into her voice.

Derek hesitated, glancing over at her again. "I like to think that we've gotten to be good friends, Sabrina, even though we haven't known each other very long. I hope you realize that I'd never do anything to make trouble for you."

"Forget it, Derek. Josh and I have a . . . an understanding. He knows that I go out with you and it doesn't bother him."

"If you were my wife I could never be that open-minded," he said softly.

She stared straight ahead. "I'd rather not discuss it if you don't mind."

He covered the clenched hand that rested on the seat between them. "Sometimes it helps if you do. That's what pals are for."

"There's nothing to discuss," she insisted. Her mouth twisted into a semblance of a smile. "Surely in your business you've come across open marriages. That's what Josh and I have."

"Was it his idea or yours?"

"It—it was a mutual decision."

"In that case, why isn't it making you happier?"

"What makes you think I'm not happy?" she demanded.
Derek pulled over to the side of the road so he could

give her his full attention. He put his hands on her shoulders, holding on firmly when she tried to pull away. "I've never stepped out of line with you and I'm not going to now, but there's something I have to say. You mean a great deal to me, honey. I really care about you."

"You're a good friend, Derek," she answered softly.

His hands tightened. "I'd like to be more than that. I've played by your rules all this time, but if there's a chance that your marriage is breaking up, I have to tell you how I feel."

She couldn't keep on pretending that everything was all sweetness and light. Derek wasn't stupid. Sabrina chose her words carefully, trying not to reveal too much. "It's true that Josh and I are having problems," she said slowly. "I don't know if we can work them out or not, but I would never . . ."

"I'm not asking you to have an affair, sweetheart. I wouldn't insult you by suggesting it. I just want you to remember that I'm waiting in the wings."

"You don't seem to give my marriage much of a chance," she said desolately.

"You were married to him once before, weren't you?" Derek shrugged. "Maybe he's just not right for you."

Did he know how long she had been in love with Josh? Still, that didn't make his statement any the less true. One-sided love wasn't the best basis for wedded bliss.

"With all the uncomplicated women in this town, I don't know why you'd want to get mixed up with me." She sighed.

His face took on a very male expression. "I'll give you three guesses."

She shook her head helplessly. "I don't indulge in casual relationships, Derek."

"That's not what I'm looking for." A spark of excitement lit his eyes. "I want to marry you, Sabrina."

She looked at him in astonishment. "You must be joking!"

He trailed his fingers down her neck. "Why does that surprise you?"

"Because you . . . we haven't . . . you've never even kissed me!"

"That's one thing we can remedy right now."

Sabrina stiffened instinctively as Derek put his arms around her. Then she forced herself to relax. Maybe this was the answer. If anything could still the awful ache of her estrangement from Josh, she was willing to try it.

But when Derek's mouth crushed hers she felt only distaste. Josh's lips were firm, his seduction slow and arousing. They savored the moment together, every deepening kiss building excitement. Derek's assault was fevered, demanding instant response. His tongue probed her mouth wetly as his hands roamed over her body with determination.

A ripple of aversion ran through Sabrina. She couldn't help remembering Josh's tantalizing caresses, lingering at each erotic area. He knew every pleasure spot on her body, and delighted in bringing her to flaming life in his arms. Sabrina groaned deep in her throat, her nails digging unconsciously into Derek's shoulders.

He drew back, looking at her with satisfaction. "Don't try to tell me we don't have a lot going for us, baby."

Sabrina felt she should explain, but she just couldn't. The pain of knowing no man could ever take Josh's place was bad enough. "I'm sorry you did that," she said quietly.

"You don't have to be embarrassed, honey." He cupped her cheek with a familiarity that was unpleasant. "Even bluebloods have normal urges." He sounded jubilant.

Sabrina considered telling him to take her home, but there was no point in precipitating a scene. Derek would fawn and beg her forgiveness, and she was unwilling to tell him the real reason for her despair. Better to go through with the evening and not repeat it.

"Can we go to the party now?" she asked in a low voice.

In spite of Sabrina's flagging spirits, the evening turned out to be entertaining. Its very novelty was interesting. The party was held on a huge sound stage. Large lights lit the festivities, illuminating the catwalks in the vast building. Delicacies had been catered in on long folding tables, and music mixed with the chatter of many voices. Sabrina was diverted from her troubles by the extroverted personalities that surrounded her.

"I want this girl for my next leading lady," Sir Frank Manning announced. "You are absolutely exquisite, my dear."

She smiled. "Unfortunately, I don't happen to be an actress."

He leaned forward to whisper in her ear, "None of the others in this town are either, but don't tell them I said so."

"I hear you've expressed that opinion to the columnists."

"That's true. Do you think it's the reason my last leading lady chewed garlic before our big love scenes?"

Sabrina smothered a grin. "It's possible, but very bad form."

"I knew you were a discerning woman! Would you consider living with me for a month or two?"

"She's spoken for," Derek advised, joining them.

"You prefer this second lead to a *star?*" the English actor thundered.

"Derek is only a friend," Sabrina explained. "I happen to have a husband."

"You wouldn't consider leaving the doddering old chap, would you?" Manning asked.

"He isn't old," she replied.

"On the physical side, is he?"

"Very. Josh plays handball and tennis regularly."

"Mmm—one of those. Probably has no sense of humor either. I hope you won't be offended, my dear, but I'm afraid we've just had the shortest affair on record."

Sabrina enjoyed the lunacy of Sir Frank and most of the other guests, forgetting herself in the immediacy of the moment. Derek brought her down to earth on the way home.

"You really fit in, Sabrina," he said admiringly. "See how great it could be?"

"Don't spoil it, Derek. I had a super time but you can't pretend that's the real world we were in tonight."

"It's *my* world and you could be part of it."

How could she tell him it was like pistachio ice cream? One lick was delicious but a whole cone would make you sick. She couldn't, of course. Sabrina tried to let him down gently.

"I had fun tonight, Derek, but perhaps we shouldn't see each other again until I get my thinking straightened out."

He pulled into her driveway and shut off the motor. "Don't say that, sweetheart! I've told you the way I feel about you."

"I'm not free to make any commitments," she reminded him.

"I'm not asking you to. Just remember that I'm here. You can always call me if you need me."

"That isn't fair to you, Derek." He was proving hard to discourage.

"You don't have to be fair. Just use me, honey," he pleaded. "I'd consider it an honor."

The glow from her happy evening was wearing off as she walked into her darkened bedroom and turned on the light. Sabrina actually jumped when she saw Josh sitting in an armchair. His long legs were stretched out and his head

158

was resting on the back of the chair, but he wasn't asleep. After her first startled reaction, she noticed that he had on a black satin robe over matching pajama trousers.

"What are you doing sitting here in the dark?" she exclaimed.

"I was waiting for you to come home."

Sabrina's nerves went on red alert, although Josh didn't seem to be angry. "Why didn't you turn on a lamp?"

He watched her nervous movements as she put her purse down and hung up her mink jacket. "I didn't need any light, I was just thinking."

Sabrina decided not to wait for his attack. "If this is going to be another of your confrontations, Josh, I'd prefer that you save it till morning. I'm tired."

"No more confrontations, Sabrina."

The way he spoke without moving was very disconcerting; Sabrina wasn't fooled. She knew about the steel muscles that were coiled under his deceptively relaxed pose.

"What are you doing here then?" she demanded.

"I'm here to tell you that you win."

"What is that supposed to mean?"

"I'll agree to a divorce."

The buzzing in her ears was suddenly so loud that she thought she hadn't heard right. "But you . . . I—I don't understand."

He got to his feet then, and it wasn't a great improvement. Now Josh was lithe and dangerous. "It's very simple. I'm giving you what you asked for."

"What changed your mind?" She forced the words through her dry mouth.

He sighed. "I suppose tonight did."

A flash of anger turned her rigid. "Because I went out with Derek without first asking if you had plans? You haven't bothered to extend me the same courtesy!"

He held his hand up. "No more, Sabrina. When I found

159

myself in the position of offering your boyfriend a drink, I knew this situation had gotten out of hand."

"He isn't my boyfriend," she muttered, not knowing what else to say.

Josh raised one dark eyebrow. "It's a more courteous term than some I could use. In any case, these arguments aren't worthy of either of us."

Sabrina looked down at her twisting fingers. "I thought you didn't want a divorce."

"I thought so too, but you've shown me there's no alternative."

"What about Grandfather? You said it might jeopardize his health."

"We'll explain it to him together the way you suggested."

She stared up at him, seeing the spiky black lashes around his amber eyes. Everything about Josh's strong face was engraved on her heart as though it would have to last a lifetime—his straight nose, his high cheekbones, the way a lock of dark hair fell across his broad forehead.

"If that's what you want," she murmured faintly.

"It isn't a question of what either of us wants, Sabrina." His sigh was almost a groan. "We've both tried, and we failed. It's pointless for us to destroy each other. You're young, you'll find someone else." He started to say something more and then changed his mind. "We'll discuss the arrangements tomorrow night. Good night, Sabrina."

She watched him go, feeling completely numb. This was even worse than the first time. At least then she had been driven by fierce emotion. This cold, clinical severing of their marriage was heartless. It left her bewildered. When the numbness wore off Sabrina knew the pain would be unbearable. She hugged her trembling body tightly, dreading the terrible moment.

CHAPTER TEN

Sabrina would always wonder afterward if she had actually caused the accident—or what would have happened if she hadn't.

Josh was already gone when she got up the next morning. Undoubtedly to avoid a lame-duck session, Sabrina thought grimly. The "arrangements," as Josh called them, might be lengthy, so they would have to wait until evening. In the meantime they had nothing to say to each other.

Sabrina was still gripped by the numbed state that had descended on her after Josh threw his bombshell. She drove to work automatically, locked her car as though it really mattered, and greeted everyone in the office pleasantly.

Fortunately it was a busy day. She took numerous phone calls, dealt with writers, and attended a lengthy editorial meeting. By concentrating on each matter as it came up, she was able to perform efficiently. Sabrina blocked off the part of her mind that kept asking frantically if there wasn't some other way to handle her own problems.

As the day drew to a close, tiny cracks began to appear in her composure. There were things to be faced, decisions to be made. She would have to rent and furnish an apartment, change her bank accounts—so many things. Driving home, Sabrina stared straight ahead, forcing herself to envision a future without Josh.

When the crash came it seemed a fitting climax to her thoughts. There was a sharp impact that threw Sabrina forward as the sickening sound of metal striking metal crumpled the right side of her car. The breath was knocked out of her and she felt a sharp pain in her temple.

Moments later her car door was yanked open and a worried man inquired, "Are you okay?"

She felt bruised and something was running down her cheek. "I think so." She started to get out of the car.

The man put his hand on her arm. "Don't move, I'll have someone call an ambulance."

Sabrina was starting to function again. Except for the pain in her head she felt all right. "I don't need an ambulance," she protested.

A crowd had gathered, including a police car. The uniformed officer helped her onto the street after she insisted. Then the ambulance arrived. The whole scene was like a bad dream.

"I can't go to the hospital; I have to get home!" She tried to make someone understand, but it was useless.

"That's a nasty gash on your forehead." The young medic led her toward the ambulance. "I think it's going to need stitches."

A long time later Sabrina convinced the hospital staff that she felt well enough to go home. They had stitched her forehead under a local anesthetic in the emergency room and given her some pills to dull the pain. The medication was making her lightheaded, but she didn't admit it to them. It didn't matter since she wasn't driving.

After paying the taxi driver, Sabrina entered the house reluctantly. The ordeal that awaited her was worse than the one she had just been through.

Josh came storming out of the den when he heard the front door open, his face like black thunder. "It's about time you got home! There's no point in putting this thing

162

off for—" He came into the hall and saw the bandage on her head. "My God, what happened?"

"I had a little accident. They insisted on taking me to the hospital and I couldn't—"

Josh reached her in a few giant steps. He lifted her chin gently. "Are you all right?"

"They took a few stitches but outside of that I'm okay, no broken bones." Her voice was still shaky. "This car came out of nowhere. I honestly don't think it was my fault, Josh."

He eased his arm around her and guided her toward the bedroom. "I'll get you into bed and call the doctor."

"I just saw a doctor," she protested. "A lot of them, in fact."

"I want a second opinion," he answered grimly. Josh carried her into the bedroom and sat her on the edge of the bed. He slipped off her jacket and started to unbutton her blouse. "First I'll make you comfortable."

He has a strange way of going about it, Sabrina thought wildly. After her blouse was open to the waist, Josh unhooked the front closure of her bra and eased both garments off her shoulders. His gentle hands were devastating on her bare body.

Sabrina wrapped her arms around her naked breasts. "Josh, please!"

His face was haggard as he stared down at her. "Don't be upset. I'm not going to touch you."

She wanted to die right then before he could hurt her any more.

Josh brought her nightgown and draped it carefully over her head, avoiding the bandage. It was easier once she was covered. Josh swiftly removed the remainder of her clothes under the concealing nightgown, then gently laid her back in the bed. It felt good to lie down, and she closed her eyes for a moment. But when Josh got up she opened them.

"Can we have our talk in here instead of the den?" she asked.

He smoothed her gilt-colored hair tenderly. "Don't think about it. Just try to get some rest."

Sabrina sat up even though it made her feel dizzy. "No, Josh, I'd like to get this over with."

The lines around his mouth deepened. "Don't worry, I won't change my mind."

"I know that," she said carefully. "I just want to get this thing settled between us. I couldn't go through another day like today."

"That makes two of us," he muttered. "But you're in no condition to discuss anything."

"There really isn't much to talk about. I don't want anything from you."

"Only your freedom?" Josh jammed his hands in his pockets. "That isn't much to show for our time together."

Sabrina tried to smile. "We had two honeymoons."

"Why couldn't they last?" Josh groaned. "All I ever wanted was to make you happy!"

"You did," she replied softly, thinking of all the times that had been sheer bliss.

"Then why do you want a divorce?" he demanded.

There was no point in reminding him that he was the one who asked for it. In all fairness, she had suggested it first. "Our whole marriage was based on deception." She sighed.

"You can't blame me for going along with Simon," he said heavily.

Sabrina's long lashes swept down. "That wasn't what I meant."

Josh sat down on the bed, clasping both of her hands. "It doesn't matter any more but I want to explain about that night with Pam." He swept on over Sabrina's feeble protests. "I did have to work that night. Simon wanted us

164

at his house for a meeting, but he got tied up at the last minute. He told me to take Pam out to dinner and bring her over afterward, which is what I did. We went to the Carriage House where your so-called friend saw us and reported back to you."

"But why did you admit it to me and then refuse to explain?" Sabrina thought that sounded just a bit too easy.

"Because I'm a fool!" His hands tightened almost painfully on hers. "I was hurt and angry that you would even suspect me of such a thing. I figured you ought to realize the whole idea was laughable. Why would I take another woman to the most popular restaurant in town if I had anything to hide?"

"I thought you were so sure of me that you didn't even bother being discreet," she whispered. "That part hurt too."

"Oh, my darling!" He framed her face in his palms, leaning forward to kiss her ever so gently on the lips. "Don't you know there's never been anyone else for me? When you left without a word I almost went out of my mind. I would have explained if I'd realized how serious it was. I suffered more than you did. Why do you think I let myself be persuaded to trick you into marriage?"

Sabrina barely heard the question. She stared at him wide-eyed, trying to digest what Josh had just told her. Such a simple explanation for such a large amount of misery! If only she'd asked instead of demanding.

When she didn't answer, the hope drained out of his face. He stood up again. "But that wasn't the only problem, was it, Sabrina? I never dreamed what else you suspected me of. There's nothing I can say to defend myself against that charge."

She had almost forgotten her other suspicions in the joy of finding out that Josh wasn't unfaithful. Now her desolation returned. Josh seemed to be admitting that he had married her for what she ultimately represented.

"Do you mean it's true?" she whispered.

"Of course it's not true, damn it!" He ran an impatient hand through his thick dark hair. "But how can I prove it? Quit my job? I'd have been willing to do that too, if I'd only known."

Her trembling mouth dropped open. "You would do that for me?"

He stared down at her, touching her cheek with gentle fingers. There was a great sadness in his eyes. "I love you so much, my darling. I would have done anything to keep you, but it's too late now. I've lost you."

"But you haven't, Josh!" It was as though a great weight had been lifted from her chest. "We can start over!"

He shook his head. "Words won't convince you, and I can't go through this again. Even if I handed in my notice tomorrow, it would take at least six months until I was out of Ameropol. I couldn't just leave them in the lurch, and it would take that long to train my successor. Somewhere along the line you would be sure I was hatching some scheme to stay on. You really want to leave me, Sabrina, and it's wrong of me to keep you against your will." He turned away, every line of his long body expressing tension. "I've psyched myself up for it now—I don't know if I could ever do it again."

Happiness flowed through Sabrina's veins like rare wine. Josh loved her! She was finally and irrevocably convinced. She got out of bed slowly and put her arms around his waist, resting her cheek against his broad back. "If you think you're getting rid of me that easily, you're very much mistaken," she murmured.

He turned around. "You shouldn't be out of bed."

"Don't change the subject." Sabrina put her arms

around his neck. "After you kiss me a few hundred times I'll go back to bed—if you come with me."

He smiled into her imploring face, kissing the tip of her nose. "The doctor would take a dim view of this kind of activity after what you've been through."

"I'm beginning to share Grandfather's opinion of those fellows," she answered disdainfully. "They frown on anything that makes you feel good."

After urging her back into bed, Josh sat on the edge, looking at her intently. "I know I can do that, my love, but is that all there is? I thought I would take you any way I could get you—I *will* take you that way. But I want so much more. I want to own your heart and your mind, not just your beautiful body."

She looked at him incredulously. "I can't believe you don't know I've been in love with you since I was ten years old."

Josh's smile was wistful. "I'm not talking about hero worship, sweetheart. I want you to love me the way a woman loves a man."

"I'm glad to find out that I'm not the only knucklehead in this family," she observed fondly. Her laughter died as she reached up to touch his strong face. "Don't you know how miserable I've been these last weeks, Josh? Do you really think I enjoyed going out with that wimp, Derek? Even he knew he didn't measure up to you."

Josh was almost afraid to believe what he was hearing. "You mean you only went out with him to make me jealous?"

"I didn't think I could," she answered somberly, remembering the hopelessness when it seemed that Josh didn't care. "I went out with him because it was better than staying home and picturing what you were doing. But I played fair with Derek. We were never anything more than friends, Josh."

"I believe you, angel." He lifted her hand and kissed the palm before holding it to his cheek. "It's the only thing that kept me sane when I was lying in that damn guest bedroom, staring at the ceiling. You don't know how often I wanted to come in here and kiss you awake so I could make love to you all night long."

"You will move back in here now, won't you, Josh? I want to be able to reach out and touch you."

"You're really determined to try my willpower, aren't you?"

"I'm trying to break it down." She grinned. But fatigue was setting in and Sabrina was starting to feel drained.

Josh tucked the covers around her lovingly. "Go to sleep, honey. I have plans for us when you're better. How would you like to go to Laguna for the weekend?"

It was a charming resort town, a pleasant drive from Los Angeles. "Oh, Josh, could we?" The prospect of a whole weekend alone with him was enchanting.

"If you stay in bed and take care of yourself. And in six months when I'm out of Ameropol we'll take our third and last honeymoon. How about the Orient this time?"

He actually meant it! Josh was willing to give up his whole career for her. She couldn't let him do it though. "You don't have to resign," Sabrina said slowly. "Just the fact that you offered is enough."

"No, my sweet." His voice was somber. "I'm never going to take a chance on losing you again. If this is what it takes it's a small price to pay."

"But what will you do? You're too young to retire."

"Afraid I won't be able to support you?" he teased. "Well, at least one of us will be working."

"I'm serious, Josh. You couldn't find another job like the one you have at Ameropol very easily."

"You're right, I couldn't," he admitted. "Maybe I'll start a consulting firm. Ameropol's stock is at an all-time high so I must have been doing something right. I'll use my knowledge to solve other people's problems."

"You *could* get a job with another conglomerate," she said tentatively. "You should at least try."

"I wouldn't do that to Simon." Josh was very definite on that point.

Sabrina looked troubled. "Grandfather depends on you so much. I don't know how he'd get along without you."

"Let me worry about that. Nobody's indispensable." He pressed her back against the pillows. "All you have to think about is getting well—and the fact that I love you."

After a good night's sleep Sabrina felt fine, except for a slight throbbing where the stitches were. She started to get up, but Josh was adamant. He called her office, explaining what had happened and leaving instructions that she wasn't to be disturbed.

Sabrina agreed just to please him. His concern was as sweet and soothing as warm honey. It was a real novelty to be completely lazy for once. She was enjoying it until the phone rang.

"Will you kindly tell me what's behind this insane notion of Josh's?" Simon didn't even bother to say hello.

"I gather he told you he's resigning," Sabrina observed dryly.

"I won't accept it," Simon roared.

"I don't see what you can do about it."

"Has he discussed this with you?" he demanded.

"Yes," she admitted cautiously.

"And you didn't try to talk him out of it?" Simon asked incredulously.

"Josh is a grown man."

"He'll be an *old* man if he goes through with this lunacy. He'll get old before he's forty! What's he doing to do with himself, sleep late and putter around the garden? It wasn't enough for *you,* so how do you think a man like Josh is going to fill his days?"

Sabrina frowned. "He won't be just sitting around the house. Josh mentioned starting a consulting business."

Simon greeted the notion with withering scorn. "That's what old men do when they get too tired or too frightened to make the decisions that have millions of dollars riding on them. Josh enjoys the challenge, Sabrina. He's used to riding the crest of the highest, most perilous wave. Do you think he's going to be happy in a little wading pool?"

Simon's argument struck a responsive chord in Sabrina. She had seen Josh in action, seen his barely restrained excitement when he was pitting his intelligence and expertise against the odds. But it was his decision, she assured herself, forcing down the doubts Simon had raised.

"I didn't know you were so poetic, Grandfather," she said lightly.

There was a heavy silence on the other end. "Talk him out of it, Sabrina. Not for my sake—for yours and Josh's."

Their conversation lasted a long time, leaving them both frustrated at the end. Simon's dire warnings made her vaguely uneasy. Long association had taught Sabrina that her grandfather would use any means to get his own way, but the mild truth in his statements was disquieting. Suddenly the pleasure went out of the lazy afternoon.

When the phone rang again she answered it eagerly, hoping it was Josh. Just the sound of his voice would chase away the shadows. But it was Derek. He had called her office and heard what happened. Although she didn't relish going through the story of the accident again, she was glad he had called. It gave her the opportunity of tying up the last loose end.

"I won't be able to see you again, Derek," she said, when he mentioned a concert she might enjoy. "Josh and I

. . . well, we've worked out our difficulties. As a good friend, I know you'll be happy for me."

He didn't sound it. "When did all this happen? You weren't too chipper when I saw you just a couple of nights ago."

She bitterly regretted letting him drag that admission out of her. "I don't think that's important," she answered coolly.

Derek was quick to react to her mood, as always. "You're right, honey, I was just surprised. Of course I'm happy for you. I think it's great!"

"Thanks, Derek. It was good of you to call."

She was preparing to hang up when he stopped her. "You know I wish you all the best, baby. But if it doesn't work out—"

"It will," she interrupted confidently.

"I hope so, but just in case," he persisted. "I want you to know that you can call me anytime. My feelings for you won't change."

Both phone calls were disturbing. Sabrina was particularly sorry she had let her relationship with Derek go on as it had. But when Josh walked in the door that night, Sabrina's spirits soared. Nothing was ever going to come between them again!

The house they stayed at in Laguna was borrowed from a bachelor friend of Josh's. It was perched on the edge of a cliff with a stunning view of the ocean. A long flight of rustic wooden stairs snaked down to a charming private beach below. It was romantic and secluded, everything Sabrina could have wished for.

But when they went to put their luggage in the master bedroom, she burst out laughing. A circular bed was positioned on a low platform facing the windows. Stereo was built into the headboard, along with electric controls to

171

open and close the heavy drapes. To top it all off, the bedspread was made of some kind of fluffy white fur.

"All this room needs is mirrors on the ceiling," she choked. "Didn't you tell your friend that you were bringing your *wife?*"

Josh grinned. "I always knew Steve wasn't loaded with class, but I didn't realize he pictured himself as the playboy of Laguna Beach."

"I wonder who decorated this oceanfront Disneyland?"

"Offhand I'd say a thirteen-year-old boy entering puberty. There's another bedroom, honey. Shall we move our things in there?"

"And give up this spectacular view? Certainly not!" Sabrina reached for the edge of the bedspread. "Things are bound to improve once I remove the abominable snowman —or whatever this thing was when it was alive." As she pulled the bedspread down they moaned in unison. "I should have known—black satin sheets!" She fell backward onto the bed, laughing helplessly.

Josh leaned over her, bracing himself on both widespread arms. "That settles it, we're sleeping in the other room! I planned on this weekend being fun, but I didn't expect to spend it in a passion pit."

As she gazed up into his rugged face, Sabrina's merriment died. She linked her arms around his neck, pulling his head down to hers. "It's been so long since we've laughed together, Josh."

"Too long." His lips barely grazed hers. "That's one of the things I've missed—along with so many others."

"Tell me," she whispered.

Their breath mingled as he murmured against her mouth, "I missed the perfume of your skin when you curled up in my arms, the little sounds you made when you responded to my touch." His husky voice deepened. "I love to watch your face when I touch you." He circled her waist with his arms, kneeling as he buried his face in her midriff. "I do know how to make you happy, don't I?"

"You always have," she answered softly.

She slid both hands inside his shirt collar, tracing the lean length of his back as far as she could reach. His groan of pleasure reverberated inside her, striking an answering chord. Twining her legs around his waist, she arched her lower body against his hard chest.

"My sweet, passionate Sabrina," he muttered thickly, pulling her shirt out of her jeans.

Josh kissed the satin skin of her stomach, circling her navel with his tongue before continuing to unfasten her blouse. His lips moved higher up her body as each button came undone. When it was completely open he unfastened her bra and ran his fingertips over each exposed breast. His tongue was both a torment and a blessing as he took each coral bud in his mouth.

Sabrina twisted under him, digging her nails into the mattress. "Please, Josh, I need you so much," she begged.

His eyes were brilliant as he stared down into her passion-filled face. "I know, my love, we need each other."

He stretched out next to her, rolling her into his arms. His mouth reached for hers almost fiercely, parting her lips for a probing kiss that demanded everything she had to give. Sabrina responded gladly, fitting her soft curves to his hard angles in an effort to experience every part of him.

Without removing his mouth from hers, Josh unsnapped her jeans and slid them down her legs. A long forefinger slipped inside the elastic of her panties, inching them down her hips until she was wild with anticipation.

"Love me, darling." She gasped.

"Yes, sweetheart." His arms tightened convulsively. "Now and always."

He left her for just a moment to fling off his own clothes, returning to kneel over her. As he stroked her flanks for a long tantalizing moment, she quivered in expectation. Then Josh filled her with intense pleasure as her body rose up to meet his. They met again and again, joined in an excitement that sent them soaring into space, propelled by a blinding explosion.

The descent was gentler as the raging fire subsided into a comfortable glow. Complete contentment wrapped them in a mutual satisfaction that needed no words.

It was a long time before Josh stirred, and then only to pull Sabrina closer. "Whatever made either of us think we could get along without each other?" he murmured.

She snuggled happily in his arms, running her hand over his muscled thigh. "I think it's called temporary insanity. Isn't it lucky we recovered in time?"

"Do you think there's any chance of a recurrence?" His hands wandered intimately over her body.

Sabrina tightened her arms around his neck, smiling up seductively. "Not for at least fifty or sixty years."

It was a night of love that surpassed either of their honeymoons. After all of the heartache and loneliness of the past weeks, they couldn't get enough of each other. Even after they went to sleep, one would awake in the starlit night, unable to resist a gentle caress that soon aroused the other.

They awoke famished after having missed dinner. Bright sunshine was streaming in the windows.

"I hope there's a restaurant nearby. I'm starving," Josh announced.

"If your tacky friend has anything but champagne and caviar in the refrigerator, I'll make breakfast here."

Josh grinned. "I thought you'd be feeling more kindly toward Steve this morning."

"Well, this bed does have its advantages," she said with a reminiscent smile. "It's such a silly shape and these sheets are so slippery that two people can't help getting very friendly in it."

Josh ran his nails lightly down her spine. "How'd you like to deepen our friendship, pal?"

She squirmed out of his grasp, laughing. "The expression 'living on love' wasn't meant to be taken seriously."

"I'm about to show you how wrong you are." He made a grab for her, which she eluded.

After breakfast they put on their bathing suits and walked down the long flight of stairs to the small crescent beach that was enclosed on both sides by tall rock formations. It was a warm sunny day, but there had been a storm at sea during the night. Giant waves were cresting high in the air, menacing everything in their path before crashing on the sand in frustrated fury.

"I guess we won't be going swimming today," Sabrina observed. "That ocean looks dangerous."

Josh's narrowed eyes were appraising the awesome display. "Not if you judge the waves correctly and dive under them at the right moment."

"And if you miscalculate?"

His intent look vanished as he turned a mischievous face to her. "Then you just have to go to plan B."

She stared at him, sensing the primal excitement he had experienced for a fleeting instant as he weighed the risks. "It's the challenge, isn't it, Josh?" she asked slowly. "Simon said you'd miss it. He even likened it to riding the waves. He said you'd never be happy in the shallows."

For an unguarded second Josh's eyes were bleak. The expression was gone almost as quickly as it had appeared. "Surely you don't take your grandfather's little games seriously? Simon says whatever he thinks will be most effective."

"But suppose he's right this time," she said uncertainly.

175

"I wouldn't ask you to do anything that made you unhappy."

"You didn't ask, it was my idea."

"You're doing it for me though, and I can't—"

He grasped her shoulders, stopping her words with a kiss. "It's all settled and I don't want to hear any more about challenges and risks. The one risk I'll never take again is losing you." He lowered her gently to the sand, settling beside her to cradle her in his arms. "Promise you'll never leave me, Sabrina," he murmured huskily.

She twined her arms around his neck, kissing the hollow in his tanned throat. "How could I?"

"I need you so." He groaned, running his hands over her pliant body. "You're like a fire in my blood."

The ocean breeze cooled their heated bodies, but nothing could quench the flame that would burn forever in Sabrina's heart. "I love you, Josh." She sighed in utter fulfillment.

CHAPTER ELEVEN

Sabrina hated to see the weekend come to a close. It had been like a romantic idyll, days and nights of total rapture. Could they hold onto this happiness once the outside world started intruding again? Sabrina tried to banish the nagging feeling of apprehension that gnawed at her.

"We can always redecorate our bedroom," Josh teased, when she expressed her reluctance to leave. "Maybe Steve could tell us where to find a round bed."

"It's an idea. Isn't there some ancient religion that believed nothing bad could happen if you stayed inside a magic circle?" She tried to speak lightly, but her foreboding was mirrored in her shadowed eyes.

"Nothing bad is ever going to happen to us again, sweetheart," Josh murmured, bending his dark head to her bright one.

Much later when they were lying lazily in each other's arms he said, "You have a big birthday coming up. How would you like me to give you a surprise party?"

"How could it be a surprise if I know about it?"

He captured her hand, kissing each fingertip. "A mere technicality. But I'm serious about the party, honey. No two people ever had more cause to celebrate."

Josh insisted on making all the arrangements. He hired the florist and the caterer, even planned the menu himself. Sabrina's only assigned duty was to buy a new dress.

177

She went through the following week in a daze of happiness, performing her duties at the office with a permanent smile on her face. The only thing that caused it to waver was the phone call from Derek. He was part of the past that Sabrina wanted to put behind her. But Derek was hard to discourage, short of being downright rude.

"What would be wrong in our having lunch together?" he asked plaintively.

"I really don't think it's a good idea," she replied coolly.

"Just a pleasant lunch for old times' sake," he coaxed.

Sabrina's patience was wearing thin. She had already refused twice. "Why would you even want to, Derek? I've told you there can't be anything between us."

"I'm fond of you, honey." He gave a little laugh. "Well, more than fond I'll admit, but all I'm asking for is your friendship."

She sighed. "You have that, Derek, but I still can't see you."

"I don't want to lose track of you," he insisted. "You mean too much to me."

"That's a very good reason for not seeing each other again."

"I wasn't pressing the point, I just want you to remember it."

Finally, in desperation she said, "I can't talk any more, Derek. I'm due at a meeting."

"Okay." He sighed heavily. "But if the time ever comes that you need me—"

"It won't," she interrupted, assuring herself as well as him.

"If it does though," he persisted, "I want you to know that I'll come running." There was something almost grim about his voice. "I don't give up easily when I want something as much as I want you."

The phone call was distasteful rather than flattering.

178

Suddenly Sabrina couldn't be certain that all Derek wanted was her friendship.

By the time the florist finished decorating that Saturday night, the house was transformed into an indoor garden. Masses of flowers perfumed the lovely rooms, and an air of expectancy pervaded the atmosphere. The new dress Sabrina had bought was a pale-green silk, draped Grecian style to leave one shoulder bare. Her long hair was caught back in a mass of curls with little tendrils escaping at the nape of her neck. As they waited to greet their guests, radiant happiness made Sabrina's face luminous.

The gracious rooms were soon filled to capacity. Sabrina and Josh were kept busy moving from one laughing, chattering group to another. The smooth flow of conversation and the way time flew by was an indication of how good a party it was.

Simon showed up very late in the evening. "Where have you been all this time?" Sabrina asked, kissing his cheek. "The party's almost over."

"Someone has to watch the store now that Josh has taken up catering as a sideline."

It was too much to expect that Simon would let an opportunity go by, but Sabrina didn't intend to get into a discussion about Josh's defection. "Please, Grandfather." She sighed. "It's my birthday."

His imperious expression softened as he reached into his coat pocket and brought out a small jeweler's box. "That's right, my dear, happy birthday."

Before she could thank him, Simon's attention was claimed by some of the other guests. After instructing a waiter to bring her grandfather a drink, Sabrina drifted off to join a different group.

It was some time later that one of the couples approached her. "We have to run, Sabrina. It was a wonderful party," the woman said. "Say good-bye to Josh for us. We looked for him but couldn't find him."

After escorting them to the door Sabrina glanced around for Josh, realizing that she hadn't seen him in a while either. She made her way through the crowded rooms without locating him. The only places left were the bedrooms. A small frown marred Sabrina's smooth forehead as she walked down the hall.

The guest-room door was open only a crack, although it should have been wide open to allow guests use of the adjoining bathroom. As she stepped closer to remedy that, the sound of voices stopped her. Josh and Simon were inside.

At first Sabrina was merely annoyed. Trust her grandfather to try to argue Josh out of resigning, even at a party! She didn't want to get involved in their discussion, but Josh was the host and people were starting to leave. As she paused indecisively, their words began to register.

"Okay, let's say I'm willing to go along with you on this latest acquisition," Simon was saying, "what's going to happen a year from now if their stock doesn't react as you predict?"

"Trust me," Josh answered confidently. "It's my job to pick companies that perform."

"I'm glad you admit your responsibility," the older man replied severely. "Either you tell Sabrina that or I'm going to. If all this nonsense about your quitting leaked out, it could damage the company."

"Stay away from her," Josh ordered. "Your meddling could ruin everything."

Sabrina's inadvertent, choked cry alerted the men. She was frozen to the spot, realizing what she had just overheard. Josh wasn't resigning from Ameropol! He and Simon were busily making long-range plans that she wasn't supposed to know about. Josh had once more succeeded in

180

disarming her completely. That was the reason for his urgent warning to Simon not to upset his careful fabrication.

If she hadn't been so utterly crushed, Sabrina could have applauded Josh's self-possession. The rueful, little-boy expression on his face when he pulled open the door might almost have been genuine.

"I'm sorry, darling." He grinned engagingly. "I told Simon this was no time to talk business, but he's determined to get his money's worth out of my last six months."

Sabrina's face conveyed her disbelief. "Don't, Josh! Don't insult my intelligence in addition to all your other sins."

His smile changed to a look of alarm. "What are you saying?"

"I'm admitting I've been a fool—something you counted on all along! You never intended to leave Ameropol. It was a grandstand play, intended to impress me." She gave a bitter laugh. "And boy, did it ever! I might have gone on believing you if I hadn't heard you just now, making plans for a year from today."

"Sabrina, you don't understand. I have to—"

"Don't bother, Josh. Your lies just aren't convincing anymore."

Sabrina ran into her bedroom, picking up her car keys instinctively. All that concerned her at that moment was a need to escape. Double glass doors led out onto a patio facing spacious green lawns. Sabrina followed the brick path that led to the garage, conscious of Josh's harsh voice calling to her.

She gunned her car mercilessly, negotiating the curved driveway with a screech of tires. It was only when she was driving down Sunset Boulevard that the crushing weight of misery hit her. Not one word Josh had ever said to her was true!

How gullible he must think her. Sabrina's hands gripped

181

the wheel as she realized that was exactly what she had been. How could she ever have believed that he would quit his treasured job for her? Why didn't she see the large escape hatch Josh had left himself by warning that it would take six months? Sabrina wondered bitterly what excuse he would have used to change his mind. It might have been interesting to watch if it wasn't all so sickening.

Sabrina had never felt so completely unloved and alone in her entire life. There was no one she could turn to. Simon was in on the whole thing, and obviously Josh had managed to convince him that his supposed resignation was a necessary ploy. It would account for the fact that Simon hadn't deluged her with the expected phone calls.

Sabrina was torn between scorching anger and abject misery. If only there was someone to pour out her troubles to. What she needed was a friend, someone who would be on *her* side for a change.

It was perhaps inevitable that Derek would spring to mind. His pledge of undying friendship and affection, although annoying at the time, had made an impression. He was exactly what she needed right now. Someone to give quiet sympathy and assurance that the world hadn't come to an end—although she knew her private one had.

She turned left at the beach, heading for Marina Del Ray where he lived. Derek had never asked her to his apartment, knowing that would be off limits, but Sabrina had heard him giving the address to someone—number eight Meadowgate. It had stuck in her memory because it was so euphonious.

The building was in a series of apartment complexes, each built around a communal swimming pool. Music and laughter were coming from many of the units, causing her a moment's concern. What if Derek was having a party? It didn't matter, she had to talk to him. Besides, hadn't he stressed the fact that he would always be there if she needed him? Sabrina put a trembling finger on the bell.

Her worst fears were realized when a tall brunette with a sulky mouth answered the door in a thin negligee. It was obvious that she wore nothing under it. Her eyes narrowed when she saw Sabrina. "What are you doing here?" she demanded rudely.

"I—I'm sorry. I must have the wrong apartment," Sabrina stammered in an agony of embarrassment.

The woman's smile was cruel as she recognized Sabrina from the movie premiere. "You've got the right place, but if you're looking for Derek, forget it."

"Who the hell is it at this time of night?" Derek's voice came from inside. "Tell whoever it is to get lost, and come back to bed."

"Does that include your girlfriend?" the woman called over her shoulder. As Sabrina started to back away she stopped her. "Don't go, Mrs. Winchester, I have something to say to you."

Derek appeared at the door, belting a short robe around his waist. His scowl changed suddenly to consternation. "Sabrina! What are you doing here?"

"That's a good question," the brunette declared angrily. "I've gone along with your crazy scheme so far, but when she starts coming here it's too much!"

"Shut your mouth!" Derek commanded. He turned pleadingly to Sabrina. "I can explain everything. Come inside for a minute."

Sabrina looked at him in horror at the tasteless suggestion. When his hand closed around her wrist, a shiver of revulsion went through her.

"She's not coming in my house," the other woman said. Her face was a mask of spite as she glared at Sabrina. "The party's over, Mrs. Rich Bitch. From now on I want you to stay away from my husband!"

"I told you to shut up!" Derek shouted, tightening his hold on Sabrina's wrist.

She stopped struggling out of pure shock, giving Derek the opportunity of pulling her inside the apartment. It was one trauma too many.

She stared at him blankly as he said, "Don't listen to her, darling. We're . . . uh . . . we're getting a divorce. I didn't tell you about Tanya because we've been separated for so long."

"I suppose I just dropped around tonight to talk about old times," the woman remarked mockingly.

"Stay out of this if you know what's good for you," Derek snarled, his eyes glittering with rage.

Tanya shrugged. "What difference does it make? Even *she's* not dumb enough to believe your lies after catching you in the act."

Sabrina could barely form the words through stiff lips. "Why, Derek? You said you wanted to be friends."

"With you or your grandfather?" Tanya asked derisively. "He figured to get to the old man through you. He said Gramps might even buy a movie studio, and then he'd be way up there. Good old pie-in-the-sky Derek. I told him it would never work."

After one look at Sabrina's face, Derek turned on his wife furiously. "You stupid broad, I ought to beat the hell out of you! I told you I'd take care of you if you cooperated, but no, you had to blow the whole thing out of the ballpark."

Sabrina didn't wait for Tanya's answer. She felt completely disoriented as she started down the steps. A hand reached out to steady her when she stumbled. She accepted it automatically, looking up into Josh's strong face.

Sabrina recoiled immediately. "What are you doing here?" she whispered.

"I followed you." He guided her out the door. "Come on, I'll take you home."

She started to protest but it didn't seem worth the effort. What difference did it make where she went—or with whom? Putting her head back against the leather seat, she closed her eyes, willing herself not to think about the ugly scene she'd just been through. It was as futile as trying to hold back a tidal wave. Had Josh witnessed this latest humiliation? Sabrina had to know, even though it was like probing a raw spot she knew would hurt.

"Were you there when . . . when they both came to the door?" she asked hesitantly.

"Yes." Josh didn't take his eyes off the road.

She turned to stare out the window. "Then you know everything."

"We'll talk about it when we get home." His low voice didn't tell her anything.

The house was dark when they got there. Sabrina wondered fleetingly what the guests had thought when both the host and hostess disappeared, but it didn't really matter now. She trailed down the hall to the bedroom where she paused uncertainly. What was she supposed to do now? Get undressed and go to bed as though nothing had happened?

"Sit down, Sabrina," Josh said gently. "We have to talk."

Her slender body stiffened. "No more excuses, Josh. Thanks to you and Derek, I don't think I'll ever believe another man as long as I live!"

"I wasn't going to offer any," he said quietly. "When you ran out of here tonight the way you did the last time, I knew everything was over for us."

"What was I supposed to do, congratulate the two of you on concocting such a clever plot?" she asked bitterly.

"If that's what you believed, I would have expected you

to ask for an explanation—perhaps even demand it, but at least wait to hear."

"That's what Derek wanted me to do." Her eyes blazed with anger. "Isn't it strange the way you both seem to think I'm feebleminded?"

Josh's stern face softened. "I'm sorry about Derek. I wish I could have saved you from that disillusionment, but you mustn't blow it out of proportion. You didn't love him, Sabrina. Only your pride is hurt."

She couldn't very well deny it. "And my faith in my own judgment," she muttered. "I really know how to pick them, don't I?"

"You didn't pick him, he picked you—as a target. Men like that who try to use women are beneath contempt."

"After all the experience I've had, you'd think I would have learned," she remarked grimly.

Josh's face paled as though she had slapped him. "I've given up trying to convince you on that score, but there's one thing I have to clear up. I *am* leaving Ameropol."

"Oh, sure! And after a glorious two-week vacation—or whatever it took to convince me—you'd have figured out some way for me to urge you to go back."

"No, I'm leaving you too, Sabrina. It's all over."

The world seemed to totter on its axis, but she managed to keep her voice steady. "At least we agree on that."

He looked at her with brooding eyes. "I'm going away. You can stay here in the house—it's yours. My attorneys will contact you about alimony. And this time I intend for you to take it," he added forcefully.

She didn't give that a thought. Only one thing registered: Josh was going away. It was something she had never envisioned. A cold hand clutched at her heart. "You don't have to leave Ameropol now that we're separating."

"I think it's best that we sever all ties," he answered quietly.

"But what about all your business plans? I thought—"

"You thought that was proof that I intended to stay," he finished for her. "Part of my job is strategic, long-term planning. I had to continue with that even though I wouldn't be there to see it through." He sighed. "It's too bad you didn't take your suspicions to Simon; he could have set you straight where I never could. You see, Sabrina, your potential block of stock was never the stepping stone you thought it was. If anything had happened to Simon, I would have been appointed to head the company—with or without your approval. I have the backing of the board of directors who would have overridden any veto you might have attempted."

"Why didn't you tell me?" she whispered.

"I have my pride too, Sabrina. If you distrusted me to that extent, then I knew our marriage had truly failed."

"But not your career! You can't throw it all away now. It's your company as much as Simon's!"

Josh's eyes were bleak. "It doesn't seem to matter anymore." He looked down at her with great sadness. Stroking her golden hair gently he said, "Good-bye, Sabrina. Take care of yourself."

Her heart was breaking as she watched him leave the room, but she knew instinctively that nothing would change his mind. Josh was convinced there was no other way.

Sabrina stayed on in the house because there was nowhere else to go. She went to work every morning and came home each night, doing her job and nothing else. From Simon she learned that Josh had left Ameropol and gone to Europe. No one knew if it was for a visit or if he intended to live there permanently.

The weeks passed but the cold lump of misery where her heart used to be didn't thaw. She was sleeping badly and she couldn't eat. Just the smell of food made her feel ill, especially in the morning. Then one day at work she fainted. A visit to the doctor confirmed what Sabrina had begun to suspect. She was pregnant.

Suddenly the world took on color again. She was going to have Josh's child! A part of him would always belong to her.

Sabrina would have kept the news from Simon as long as possible, but he found out inadvertently. He was so worried about how wan she looked that he called the doctor, who didn't realize that Sabrina didn't want her grandfather to know.

"This is wonderful, sweetheart!" Simon exclaimed when he confronted her with the news. "Now you and Josh can settle down and forget all of this off-again, on-again lunacy."

"No, Grandfather! I don't want Josh to know," she said sharply.

He looked at her incredulously. "Are you out of your mind, child? You can't exactly keep this a secret."

"I can for as long as possible—especially with Josh in Europe." Tears filled her eyes but she refused to let them fall. "I'm not going to use this baby to force him to come back to me."

"Oh, for—!" Simon controlled himself with an effort. "Josh left here a broken man. He loves you so much it's killing him! If you had any sense you'd know that he'd jump at any chance to come back."

Sabrina refused to let herself hope for the impossible. "You're not to tell him I'm pregnant," she said somberly. "Promise me."

"I can't let you—"

"If you don't promise, I'll go away and you'll never see me *or* your great-grandchild," she said sternly.

188

After looking hopelessly at her taut figure and determined face, he sighed heavily. "All right, I promise."

Sabrina had just gotten undressed the next night when she heard a car door slam. Looking out of the window, she saw Simon's limousine in the driveway. The last thing she wanted was another round with her grandfather, but she couldn't very well pretend she wasn't home. After putting on a robe, she went to the door. When she opened it Sabrina turned pale. Josh was standing under the entry light.

He caught her as she swayed. "What is it, darling? You do look sick! What's the matter?"

She could only stare at him mutely, noticing the deep lines in his face that hadn't been there before. He was thinner too, making his high cheekbones more prominent. But his supple body was the same, the ultimate in masculinity.

"Josh has just flown thousands of miles to see you," Simon declared. "Are you going to keep him standing on the doorstep?"

Sabrina's heart had started to beat again. She turned reproachful eyes on her grandfather. "How could you? And after you *promised!*"

"I didn't tell him that you were—you know." His face was wreathed in smiles. "Well, I'll leave you children alone. I know you have a lot to talk about." He beat a hasty retreat to the waiting limousine.

"What's going on?" Josh looked both worried and baffled. "Simon called and told me you'd been to the doctor and I'd better get home right away." He was very pale under his tan. "It isn't anything serious, is it, Sabrina?"

She sighed. "No, it's not serious."

He gripped her shoulders. "Don't keep anything from me. Whatever it is, we'll get the best doctors."

189

"I'm not sick, Josh," she insisted. "Simon had no right to call you home. You mustn't feel responsible for me."

"Is that why you think I came?" He crushed her in his arms so tightly that she could feel every remembered muscle. "If anything happened to you I couldn't go on living! I missed you so much that sometimes I actually hoped I'd die and get the agony over with."

She started to tremble. "You've forgiven me for all my doubts and suspicions?"

He looked at her with such yearning that Sabrina felt herself melt inside. "I'd forgive you for anything if you'd only love me again."

"I never stopped," she answered softly.

"Oh, my darling!" Josh's mouth closed over hers with a wild, sweet hunger. He held her as though he would never let go. "I was so lonely for so long." His hands wandered over her back before wrapping tightly again around Sabrina's slim body. "You'll never know the hell I went through without you."

She rubbed her cheek against his broad shoulder, inhaling the wonderful male aroma of him. "I went through the same hell until I found out—" She stopped abruptly. The news she had was too glorious to be blurted out in the entry hall.

Josh drew back to look at her searchingly. His hands gripped her shoulders hard. "Found out what? You have to tell me what's wrong."

"Come in the bedroom," she said gently.

"Don't try to spare me, Sabrina!"

She shook her head, taking his hand and tugging him gently down the hall.

When they were in the bedroom he pleaded with her. "Whatever it is, we'll face it together, darling. I never should have left you." He groaned. "This is all my fault!"

She gave him a bewitching smile, linking her arms

190

around his neck. "I'm glad you realize that you're responsible."

"I'll do anything, my love—anything at all!"

"You've already done your part." Her face was radiant as she took pity on him. "I'm going to have a baby."

It took a moment to sink in, and then Josh's eyes blazed with incredulous joy. He swept her into his arms, holding her tightly while he got used to the idea. "Why didn't you tell me, sweetheart? Why didn't you call me instead of Simon?"

Sabrina moved out of his arms, going over to sit on the edge of the bed. "I didn't want to blackmail you into coming back to me, Josh. I still don't."

He stood over her, raising her face to his. "I want this baby very much, my dearest, but I want you more. Will you take me back?"

She smiled through her tears. "For all of my brave talk, I don't think I could let you go if I tried."

Josh's kiss was very tender as he lifted her onto the bed and settled beside her. His caresses were gentle, wandering over her body as though becoming reacquainted with a lost treasure. Sabrina did the same to him, unbuttoning his shirt so she could tangle her fingers in the crisp hair on his lean chest.

The slow contentment grew into a warm tide that swept through both of them. Josh's kiss deepened in sensuality, his tongue exploring her mouth as his hands started to explore Sabrina's body. Her soft cry of delight spurred him on and he slipped the gown from her shoulders, trailing a line of fiery kisses between her breasts. She opened his shirt to the waist and unbuckled his belt. Her hands wandered over his body, discovering how great his passion was.

Their union was a thing of joy and celebration, an affirmation of love and trust. Sabrina's body was swept by wave after wave of pulsing sensation, culminating in a burst of power that left her filled with rapture.

Much later when they were lying peacefully entwined, she said, "I suppose Grandfather will expect you back to work tomorrow morning."

Josh stirred in her arms. "You know better than that. I'm not going back, Sabrina."

"Of course you are. *I'm* not going to be the sole support of this child."

"No, darling." His arms tightened a little desperately. "I wouldn't jeopardize what we have for a million jobs."

"If you're worrying about that pesky stock—don't," she said casually. "I've decided what to do with it. I'm going to ask Simon to leave it in trust for little Joshua Junior."

Josh's tense body relaxed as he looked into her serene face. "Don't you mean little Sabrina?"

She kissed the tip of his nose. "Keep a good thought—maybe we'll have twins."